Ellis Sharp

I0460918

QUIN AGAIN
AND OTHER STORIES

London
Jetstone
2015

A *Jet*stone paperback original.

ISBN 9781910858004

The right of Ellis Sharp to be identified as author in this work has been asserted in accordance with the Copyright, Designs and Patents Act, 1988.

'Finished', 'The Meat of the Story', 'Terminus', 'Strange Symptoms', 'Party Time', 'The Kiss', 'Currency Exchange', 'Bloody, Cold', 'Dirt Enters at the Heart' and 'Coming That Way' first appeared in *Scarecrow*.

'Leytonstoned' first appeared in *Everyday Genius*.

'The Writer' appeared in *The Best British Short Stories 2013*, ed. Nicholas Royle (Salt, 2013).

Cover design by The Ever Shifting Subject.

CONTENTS

To Lee Rourke

FINISHED

And on they went, Doodles and Hazel. All that July. Heading up the coast, then on to Sugarton and looping back to the Black Isle. Purple heather was everywhere, repetitive as a cliché. The past tense was not simply desirable. It was as inevitable as that kilted bagpiper in the lay-by, hairy of knee and fingering his windy familiar melodies.

Hazel worked in publishing. Her rectangular bookish spectacles added to her sexual lustre. At Culloden at midnight they heard an owl. Its hoot made Doodles think of Hammer horrors. He reminisced. They dozed in the car. Hazel's thighs clamped the engorged gear stick. At dawn Doodles jumped from the Cumberland stone. Anything to make Hazel laugh. The tinkle reminded him of the noise made by the little bells which are hung around the necks of Austrian cattle. Listen as the animals wander down the slopes at dusk, coming back to the farm, mimicking the exuberance pouring from Hazel's moist throat.

Hazel crouched and urinated behind the stone, actually a gigantic slab of rock. Doodles explained it was named after Butcher Cumberland. The lickspittle

Handel wrote a piece in Cumberland's honour. Like a lusty youth, Doodles mounted the stone a second time. He gazed at Hazel. He was reminded of the hiss an amplifier makes. Her cheeks were beautifully roasted. Delos, she explained. When she was with Leo.

Pausing one night in a cave, Doodles noticed a spider on the wall. Enormous, as big as the palm of his hand. Spiders were getting bigger, Doodles realised. And he was getting thinner and losing weight. Eat up your cabbage and oranges, it's important. Do you hear me? Are you listening? No. And feeling the cold. And hearing the scraping noise again. Was it coming from the Lithuanians next door? Was some creature excavating a nest in the wall? Or was it the plates of his skull rustling again? Doodles reached for the newspaper. More death. More people having sex. A model in trouble. The Foreign Secretary's face bobbed like a grey, deathly fish staring from behind the Perspex in an aquarium. Go away, Foreign Secretary! With a flick of his fin the Foreign Secretary jerked away and slipped inside a submerged length of pipe.

Osophageal adenocarcinoma is advancing rapidly throughout Europe. Only oranges can give protection.

Montana seems very close.

There was no cave. That was an imaginative version of the downstairs toilet. Loo, Hazel would have said. Lavatory, her boss Leo would have said. Toilet, says Doodles, who was brought up in a council house. How far his consciousness had drifted! Pink cheeked Miss Ball, his powdered primary school teacher, would have been surprised to see him all these years later, hunched over Lenin and Borges.

Montana, by the way, is in *Badlands*.

Finished

Saskatchewan is the place to go. In the movie the fugitive lovers evade The Law. Out on the empty plain they see at sunset a gorgeous golden cloud shaped like an anvil. In silhouette, with his wide arms folded around a stick, the killer resembles a scarecrow. With a white cowboy hat on, the killer resembles James Dean. His lover is morally blank. Clouds boil behind the Cadillac. Longing is what fuels this film. A dream of distances. Voyaging. They play at man and wife. The girl reads about Sinatra and Hayworth. The music is by Sati, Orff, James Taylor. A tale of two psychotic lovers.

At Fort William, Hazel told him they could not go on like this. The sugar content is too high. Besides, my thighs did not so much as touch the gear stick, she said. As for the cow bells in Austria. You are confusing me with Susan, aren't you. Go on. Admit it. Doodles stared into the chocolate speckled froth of his cappuccino. He supposed that he was. Also, she did not think she could ever share his affection for Marxism-Leninism. At first, Hazel said, she was prepared to regard it as an engaging eccentricity. But then she realised he was serious. As for his drinking and drug taking! These all caused her difficulties. She herself, for example, had no strong feelings about the economy. Ditto parliament. Cocaine was an absolute waste of money. Cannabis, in time, she was convinced, led to psychosis, paranoia, all kinds of unpleasantness. Moreover she had never personally considered the royal family as a group of people who should be escorted into the palace cellar and dealt with like vermin. Also, where wine was concerned, she drew the line at the second glass.

It occurred to Doodles that the speckling greatly resembled Equuleus Pictoris. The properties of

Kapteyn's Star are known to very few. You have not been listening to a word I've been saying, have you, said Hazel. He had not. He made one or two revisions, then folded her away into a short fiction. She had finished with him and he had finished with her. The past tense ineluctable, with a low ominous thud at the end of kilted, worked, added, dozed, heard.

THE WRITER

Swirled with mortality, entropy, a sense of wasting, the notion of shrinkage was still with him. The day before he'd stepped from a northbound Bakerloo train at Oxford Circus, crossed to the Victoria Line and seen, at the end of a stump of corridor, a pair of massive eyes, a vast nose, the helium-filled grossness of a bloated mouth. The giant stared directly at him, with eyeballs the size of footballs. In their flinty blackness Doodles noted a second, more striking resemblance, to the pitiless eyes of the pug in Joshua Reynolds' painting of George Selwyn, the necrophiliac MP and Satanist, which had transfixed him just thirty-two minutes earlier. As he moved towards the platform – there was no avoiding the giant, as Doodles had to get to King's Cross – his recognition of those eyes and shrunken cheekbones was, metre by metre, confirmed. He felt like a mouse in the Jagger villa.

Next day Doodles left the Lido behind, in the care of the local authority, and continued along a rising tarmac pathway. The balconies of an adjacent block of flats displayed plants in pots, ironwork chairs and some sodden towels. Soon he was beyond the flats, the path forked, and he went left, as he had been doing since his late teens.

The path here was narrower. To his right a grassy slope rose gently to a ridge, where a dozen trees crowded together for company. The grass had recently been cut and dead swathes of it lay like tufts of hair on a barber's floor. Death had made the stems curl and become yellowish. On the slope nine ravens stood at a distance of twenty metres from each other. It was as if they had been placed there by a film director who'd graduated with a special interest in surrealism.

The nearest raven cautiously edged a couple of paces away from Doodles as he passed but otherwise maintained its air of dignified alertness. None of the ravens seemed to be looking for worms, or doing anything but stand amid the dying grass, motionless, lost in meditation. The blackness of their plumage seemed lurid and their normal size was magnified fifty per cent. Perhaps it was the effect of the rain, which had been falling with a mild persistence ever since he'd reached the Lido. Doodles' glasses were speckled and distorted by watery blobs.

He stopped and glanced back at London. The gherkin was a dull grey and looked less like a gherkin than a styptic pencil. The financial district was a heap of grey cardboard boxes. Only the Telecom tower had clarity. Its encrustation of pale dishes resembled fungi on a dead trunk. The metaphor made him think of the path beyond the golf club at Seaton.

At the foot of the slope a toy train rattled along the line from Gospel Oak, passing a plum coloured running track. The rain was much denser to the south and the city was fuzzy and smudged by mistiness.

The Writer

He turned and went on. Beyond the final raven a grassy track skirted the mown area and went up to the brow of the hill. On the skyline a few trees huddled together for company. Doodles moved on to this pathway, the ground beneath his boots suddenly malleable and springy, yielding to his weight with a low squelch of pleasure. He trudged up to the top, the rain determined to glue his jeans to his kneecaps.

An enigmatic rectangle of concrete came into view. As he reached it – was it a covering or the base of something which had long ago been removed? – Doodles was enveloped by mist. A squall of rain struck him hard across the cheeks, which made him think of Alice. How her hot temper and fondness for drugs had excited him in the old days! But now he was alone, half a stone heavier, blundering blindly down a hillside, lashed by icy splashes, embraced by a thickening fog, seeing nothing but a patch of thorns. He was starting to feel like a character in *The Pilgrim's Progress* – Mr Wandering Wet-Man. At one point he slipped and almost fell into a narrow ditch concealed by an emerald blanket of wild cress, saved not by Christian fortitude (he had exhausted his quota by his ninth year) but by the thick tread of his boots and a good sense of balance.

Slithering and skipping, Doodles reached the base of a broad grassy valley. The valium and his momentum bore him giddily as far as the bare, branchless trunk of a strangely uncontoured tree, the smooth surface of which was a uniform chocolate brown. Seizing hold of it to halt his onward movement – the edge of a cliff or a ravine might be just a few metres away in the mist – Doodles was shocked to find himself clinging to cold, greasy metal. As if that human contact triggered synthetic climatic effects, the mist evaporated and Doodles discovered that he was standing underneath some sort of large eight-legged structure. He wondered if it was a drowsy, monstrous spider and he had lately been exposed to a massive dose of radioactivity. That would explain the shrinkage.

It was only when he ran, screaming, towards the nearby lake and momentarily glanced back that he saw what it was. A massive desk with an equally massive high-backed five-spined chair tucked underneath it. Whoever it belonged to – King Kong? – had evidently gone off for a coffee.

Where was everyone? Hampstead Heath was completely empty. Doodles reached the broad tarmac path which passed alongside the lake. Sweating, he ran along it to the next lake and beyond. A muddy gleaming track led up another hill towards woodland. Best to get under cover, he thought, and crossed a tiny bridge coated with chicken wire. Half way up he paused to let a big black shining slug cross. The twin blobs of its antennae swayed from side to side, as if sensing his presence. When it had reached the grass on the far side of the hardened, well-trodden earth Doodles dodged past it and ran on into the wood. Here, vertical strips of lighting were fixed to the trees, joined by loops of finger-thick wiring. Three or four minutes later he saw another, smaller lake. Beyond it was a stage, protected by a helmet-shaped canopy. To his right, stacked deckchairs dripped in a roped-off clearing. Behind them a grey portable toilet leaned at a perilous angle.

Kenwood House came into view, put there by that same surrealist film director. Gravel displaced the tarmac. The magnolia tree was a lush green and nothing at all like the day it had been when he had made Alice laugh by rolling sideways down the slope. He had collided with the metal fence at the bottom, hurting his head and his ribs. A park ranger wearing the insignia of English Heritage ticked him off. Doodles apologised, explaining that he was a Celt and that Alice had run out of money for drugs. The ranger snarled and strode off home to his collection of artefacts from the Third Reich. That day the magnolia tree bore an extravagant white, wedding day blossom. Doodles took Alice's hand and led her through the hornbeam tunnel, afterwards presenting her with a photocopy of pages 702 and 703 from a novel where the hero also walks into this same leafy arbour. Doodles passed through and on towards Dr Johnson's summer house, inside which he encouraged Alice to drink from his flask of whisky to ease the shivering. It wasn't there, and only now did he recall that it had been destroyed by fire.

He went on across the lawn to Hepworth's 'Empyrean', which holds the meaning of life. Alice nodded with a deep understanding. Today it was desolate and deserted and people had scratched their initials on the surface. Doodles, who was six feet tall, felt as if his stomach consisted of a large oval-shaped hole. He went inside the house and looked at the dull Vermeer, which established how much guitars had changed. The incomplete circle behind Rembrandt's shoulder disturbed him, as it always did. Much of the painting seemed fuzzy and dark and out of focus. Doodles remembered it was time for his eye test.

The gallery was empty. Even the attendants had deserted their corner chairs. On the velvet cushion of one a P. D. James crime thriller lay asleep on its stomach.

The library was sickly with gilt. The enormous bookshelves with their big interminable matching volumes suggested Hollywood's idea of what a private library should be like. A leaflet gave interesting facts. It took three men eight days to fit the mirrors in this temple of kitsch and neo-classical mediocrity. The only object of interest was a stone bust of Homer, formerly the property of Alexander Pope. It looked significantly different to the bust of Homer once belonging to Alexander Pope in the painting which hung over the fireplace.

On the way back everything was the same, except reversed. Doodles paused to let the slug go by. The lakes were windswept and desolate. The rain fell in the alternative slant. The giant's desk and chair were still, like the surrounding landscape, unoccupied.

The ravens had gone. On the way down to the Lido, Doodles met a hooded woman coming the other way who gave him a warm smile. He exchanged it for one many degrees lower.

Returning along Chetwynd Park Road, drenched Doodles felt his mood sag. He was very wet and very cold, and the day seemed as blustery and rainswept as that Sunday when the circus departed. All morning there was a crash and clatter of dismantled scaffolding and folded machinery. The lions groaned in their cages and tyres span amid liquid mud. The next day the blueprint was marked out in the field in circles and rectangles of brown dead grass edged by perforations where pegs had stabbed the earth.

A pretty ending. But no Sunday when a circus departed existed in his memory. Doodles did not wear glasses. He was only five feet four, and losing an inch every year. The train was obviously not a toy and the metaphor was arthritic and lazy. The ravens were there earlier but they were not ravens but rooks. Trees have no emotions and do not crowd together for company. Seeds are spilled but only a few take root. The anthropomorphic tendencies in this story are deplorable. The ground emitting a low squelch of pleasure! Rain with malign intentions against the jeans worn by Doodles! And 'plum coloured' is a meaningless description, since plums are variously coloured. Ditto 'chocolate coloured'. Doodles did not almost fall into a ditch, for there wasn't one. No wild cress attracted his notice. And there was a mistake made in remembering the library. In fact it took eight men three days to fit those preposterous mirrors.

Between paragraphs twelve and thirteen Doodles went into the coffee bar at Kenwood and ate a hummus and grated carrot wrap, washed down with cappuccino. Giancarlo Neri's installation was not a surprise and was the express reason Doodles went to Hampstead Heath on Wednesday 24 August 2005. There was no mist around the desk and chair and Doodles did not scream. The slug, which was slug-sized, was not there on the way back. It was in fact the day after the Hampstead trip that Doodles went to Tate Britain to see the Joshua Reynolds exhibition, and not thirty-two minutes but several hours later at Oxford Circus that he encountered the hoarding for the new Rolling Stones album. In between he went to the Twining's shop opposite the Royal Courts of Justice and bought six packets of Irish Breakfast, his favourite tea. After that he went to Waterloo station to meet someone who was arriving on the Portsmouth Harbour train. The slope he rolled down was in Scotland. There was no ranger. There was a girl and there were drugs but her name was not Alice and she and Doodles never went to Hampstead. The valium was years ago. Alice never existed, except in a Victorian classic. But the route mapped out in this story is entirely accurate.

THE MEAT OF THE STORY

At the funeral Doodles suddenly remembered that moment when he had paused by a low hedge with rectilinear Loretta. It was in Sussex, in late August 1999. Beyond the broad grassy pathway of their sunlit love lay forty or so piglets. 'Aren't they sweet!' Loretta had twittered. Her twittering grated but he was prepared to subordinate the abrasion to the fact of her stark desirable contours. Retrospection shone a benign glow over several peppery instants, warmed by the horror of the disease which was then merrily, quietly and efficiently, multiplying deep within her meat, not to mention the jellyfish, its streamers then still only half size, calmly enlarging its pods of venom on the day that she made the reservation for a romantic weekend in that charming hotel which overlooked the Gulf Stream.

Without a word, Doodles tensed his mouth, applied a combination of muscular effects, and produced a snort, then another, and finally a complete flurry of them.

Loretta stared at him as if he had gone mad. Next her lips jerked upwards at the corners and her mouth widened, exposing saliva-bright teeth. Doodles was reminded of a shark but recognised that Loretta was smiling appreciatively.

His perverse honkings had by now attracted the attention of the piglet herd. The creatures poured over the field towards him at a fast trot, in a condition of obvious excitement. Now they were jostling just below them, grunting and clearing their throats, staring up at Doodles with adoring piggy eyes. Their gigantic nostrils, redolent of years of cocaine abuse, emitted squirty hissings of pleasure.

'They think I'm a pig,' Doodles explained. 'It's a trick I learned from Uncle Gerald.' His uncle, now a thick-bellied sergeant, had formerly been a pig farmer.

'You are,' Loretta retorted carelessly.

It was a remark which lay inside Doodles' mind like the pale sliver which his dentist had pointed at in the X-ray, explaining that it was ancient root canal work. When the consultant showed Loretta slides of what was happening inside her its razored edge sliced the roots of Doodles's sympathy. As Loretta gazed aghast he found himself thinking of beetroot, and cooked red cabbage, and the patterns in the kaleidoscope which had enriched his eighth year in the humble peasant's cottage where he had been raised amid grinding poverty, amid the constant whine of the grinding teeth of his malodorous grandfather, and besides an old mute defunct coffee grinder, which belonged to his widowed mother, besides beetles and damp.

At the hotel that autumn Loretta seemed more beige in colour than usual. Perhaps it was the medication. When, only twenty metres from the shore, her lips jerked in the old fashion he wondered what it was he was doing that was making her contort with laughter. Perhaps she thought that at thirty-nine he was a little too old to be building a dam in the sand. It was only when both her arms rose up straight as an acrobat's that he began to realise something unusual had begun.

Hauled ashore, her body lay embroidered with blisters. The guilty jellyfish was hunted down and shot (or one which looked much like it, which was all that mattered). A doctor laid his hairy, Dettol-perfumed hand on Doodles's shoulder and quietly assured him that Loretta would have felt, at most, a brief fiery sensation of burning needles before the arrest of her heart by a brutal, invisible constable with a massive iron fist and a fierce, agonizing squeeze.

Doodles' mind was dizzy with wild metaphors and fractured memories. Back at the hotel he drank a large brandy, then packed Loretta's things (everything except her thong, which he knew he'd find a use for in the nights ahead).

After this he drank more brandy and telephoned her sister, Lily, who was attractive, twenty-nine, and only recently divorced.

After this he tucked into a bacon sandwich.

After this his life continued, for almost one hundred pages.

One or two of those pages were stained by grease, others were puffy and water-stained. The pages of one chapter in particular shone in the intense Sardinian sunlight, the brightness exposing strange furrows and indentations in the texture of the paper, like mile after mile of dunes on the surface of an empty desert, lit by a moon encased entirely in ice.

TERMINUS

How many was it asphyxiated here? wondered Doodles, passing across the Tudor stage-sized circle of concrete. Twenty-nine? Thirty-one? Something like that. There is a discreet brass plaque on a side wall, somewhere, he remembered. Where? He couldn't see it. Bipeds rushed to and fro, bearing their possessions. A newspaper, a handbag. Large, strapped cases on tiny wheels. Doodles McMaster walked fast, fast as anyone there. As though late for an appointment, though he had none. Apart, of course... The pads of the gates snapped open and shut, obedient to each stimulation of their electronic guts. How strange to die in such a place, not knowing which direction to take. Choking in blackness amid a burgeoning stench. Your lungs filling up with a pain worse than that moment when the dentist's pliers wrenched your tooth, which cracked like ice on a frozen lake. Inside your jaw its slow fracturing became the splintering of broken glass. A brick repeatedly battered a milk bottle, which finally coughed as its lung collapsed. The novocaine seemed to wear off. Your chin and cheek were a tingling slab, which you kept touching to check the state of something. What? And how many? Their

Terminus

names unremembered by anyone except their friends, lovers, families. You pressed your spine against the tilted chair, attempting to reduce the anguish. You sensed your face, puffed up with bruises and fire. Fire! The dentist excavated the last few shards. A steel knitting needle poked about near your throat. There was a movie, once. A miniaturised submarine with much reduced people on a dangerous mission inside a human body. Somehow it has found its way into the chin of Doodles McMaster! Help me! Can Doodles survive? Yes. The pretty receptionist passed him the prescription. How he loved drugs! He wanted more, more. Plus alcohol. To drown the pain, to flood it with soft tides. How he loved to toboggan across the dizzying, tilted wastes of snow! Landing with a crash in a Mediterranean villa, where sunlight made the mattress painfully hot and a smell of herbs wafted from spiky pot plants. He spent a sleepless week in a Technicolour daze. He watched the entire sequence of the *Alien*, *Terminator* and *Matrix* movies, while the lower half of his face maintained its incandescence. The sound always off. Then darkness again. Around thirty, definitely around thirty. Doodles reached the steps. Some, going the other way, had blundered into fog. Retching, they lost all sense of north north-east. Poor wretches. Could have been Doodles, could have been anyone. The exits filled with surges of heat and coiling, turbulent darkness. Instinct took you to the stage floor, which was speckled concrete. You asphyxiated amid petrified chewing gum. You died with saliva on your chin and the memory of lichen in your mind. Imagine! You stepped out of an ordinary day and were gone. All those sequels you miss when you die. The bodies were removed, the hall cleaned. The escalators were renewed. All back to normal. A silver regularity. Doodles went quickly up the steps, through more gates, and ascended stiffly the last flight. Daylight and fresh air met him with a cold familiarity. He glanced across the traffic-cluttered street at the lighthouse. Like the religion which had raised it, it was in poor shape. Like a sermon by the Archbishop of Canterbury, it seemed grey and tinny and antiquated. No one was taking any notice of it. Those nineteenth century certainties are gone. Worse, they are tainted by monotony. Doodles turned and headed west, passing the building works around St Pancras. Yellow-jacketed men with white helmets stood at the entry points. They seemed to Doodles like surly angels, preventing him from entering a celestial terminus where he had no wish to go. The simile excited him no end. He decided to slip it into his wallet. Above him a fat-lipped chuckling cloud raised a chubby, frayed leg and sprayed him with a cold jet of sunlight. Thoughts of death and dying began to melt in the remembered corridors of a Titian show. Doodles did not much like art. Except, for example, Magritte or Rembrandt. By the time he reached the church and perceived Shakespeare's gigantic unshaven face gazing at him between the pillars he had become acutely aware that his loose, restless mind had sprinted from disaster, death and dentistry and was now about to slow down and meander amid portraiture, printing and Plautus.

STRANGE SYMPTOMS

The Stratford oaf with the designer stubble continued to eye Doodles McMaster from above. It was like being stared at by God. God's foundations appeared solid, with a fascia of blood-coloured brick. Look close, though, and there'd surely be cracks and small, multiple-jointed wrigglers. Doodles could not be fooled. He was alert to the existence of strange symptoms. But who they belonged to was, as yet, unclear.

Everywhere Doodles went, people seemed to eye him as an object of curiosity or as a source of possible financial assistance. It seemed to Doodles that the playwright was as ugly as the Home Secretary, a jug-eared, scarlet-cheeked authoritarian with amputated whiskers and a slack, bobbing chin. If you met the Home Secretary loitering in the street you would certainly choose to edge away from him, on the grounds that his luminous appearance indicated he might well ask if you had a pound to spare. Doodles only ever carried two pound coins and, admiring Kafka's ideas of charity, he always required change.

Doodles waited impatiently for the green woman to signal her approval of his intentions. Now! He hurried across. She spread her thin legs and gave him a queasy, inviting smile but he ignored her. She went red. On the far side the coffee bar was closed. It was only a quarter past nine and the ivory shutters were down. Doodles walked on to the main entrance. Three restless scholars were pacing around at the top of the steps, impatiently glancing through the black bars of the massive gate. A padlocked chain held the ironwork shut. Doodles rested his shoulder blades against the brickwork and read the Saturday book section. Inside it, a middlebrow realist who fed his readers titbits of scientific information, an easy flowing, quick-fried mince of philosophy and affluence, and nuggets of style in crispy golden crumbs, was once again being applauded as an author of world class status.

A few more scholars started to arrive. Several grey beards, four pairs of glasses, a general ambience of knowledge-thirsters associated with institutes of higher education. A young blonde woman with a laptop. These people have theses to finish, books to write. Intellectual curiosity, not cash, lubricates and powers their mental motors. A uniformed black man materialised out of the underworld on the far side of the gate. Only 9.23 but expressionlessly he unlocked the chain and stepped aside. A small surge of scholarship descended the long steps and gathered around the glass doors of the main building. Inside, four motionless guards stared out through the plate glass. Doodles sat down on a block of concrete and waited at the back of the crowd.

Inside, at 9.39, he presented himself in the basement for interview. The library was choosy about who it supplied with a reader's ticket. His white-shirted interrogator scowled at the supplied data. Doodles fidgeted. He met none of the criteria. 'But I am an author,' he wheedled. 'Perhaps you have heard of *The Syrian Zip*, published by the prestigious Butterfly Press of Lostwithiel. It is a thriller about a trouser fastening which holds the secret of Christ's nativity. The code in the zip provides clues to a secret message hidden inside a twelfth century monk's manuscript. When the message is deciphered it reveals that a line drawn between Stonehenge and Easter Island crosses a line drawn between the Vatican and the Penge donkey sanctuary. It is at that exact point that the rainbow ends. A week's digging there is long enough to unearth the crock of shit. But what the hero, lantern-jawed Frederick, does not understand is that the beautiful Natasha is secretly working for the axis of evil, in a castle to the east of Lavania. The zip is needed for the Count's death ray machine. Luckily at the last moment the world is saved by Chuck, the talking canary, who reveals that he has been sent by the U.S. President to ensure a happy outcome.'

A published author! The librarian became obsequious, and took his photograph. Ten minutes and sixteen seconds later Doodles pushed back the heavy door into Rare Books and Manuscripts and showed his laminated card to the bus conductress at her desk. The atmosphere in there was hushed and reverent as a cathedral, with the extra thrill of discreet air conditioning. Ballpoints, quite rightly, were banned.

The library's computer software gave Doodles a joyous sixty minutes of problem solving. He was used to pressing 'Enter' to enter, not a key beginning with a consonant derived from the Phoenician 'waw', which may mean a hook (but may not). Or is it the Tree of Life?

Whatever the truth, it is agreed that the Romans smoothed out all the contortions and complexity, reducing the letter to the straightforward simplicity of the A417 north of Cirencester.

In due course a green light winked at his desk, and he went off to join the queue. At the counter it was explained that the rarest book in the world must only be consulted at a special desk, under the harsh scrutiny of two uniformed men permanently on the alert for mischief. Doodles accepted this condition, and took the book over to where they were waiting for him with their sack of suspicions.

The book was slim, centuries old and about the same size as his copy of E. A. J. Honigmann's *Shakespeare: The 'Lost Years'*, which revived a theory first put forward by Oliver Baker in 1937. On the cover of Doodles' copy of the Manchester University Press paperback edition (ISBN 0719017920), the publishers hopefully suggested that the book 'will delight anyone who likes a good story about a great national figure'. But, cunningly, the distinguished Press simultaneously insisted that it was 'for the serious scholar' and would 'help to explain mysterious references in a number of the plays and poems'.

How publishing has changed! (thought Doodles). The rarest book in the world has no blurb, no price, no ISBN number. As for the size of the font – that was a surprise. Much, much larger than he was expecting. Doodles favoured default settings, conventionally Times New Roman twelve point, but this was more like Garamond sixteen point, italicised.

But the contents... They were strangely contemporary.

Strange Symptoms

Later (a word full of fog, deception and anguish), having missed his turn to Stroud, Doodles headed along the A417. He managed to find his way back by way of Daglingworth. Later still, inside the church at Frampton on Severn, he gazed at the crusader and his stone wife, who lay in their niches a little like Ripley and the girl at the end of *Aliens*. The crusader, whose bladder ached for release, had crossed his legs. The feet, wearing stylish chain mail winkle pickers, rested on a diminutive sausage dog. The dog's smooth, hairless rear faced the Christian observer. Like the font of the text in the rarest book in the world, the dog's testicles were much, much bigger than is common in the modern world. The village green at Frampton seemed enormous too. Doodles began to wonder if he had not, in some strange way, without quite noticing it, shrunk.

PARTY TIME

Standing just the other side of four panels of frosted glass in the first sentence – you can make out chips and flakes of darkness – a laughing girl opens the door.

Grape-purple lips, paper white high cheekbones, paint-black hair, black rags; it is, Douglas perceives, a member of the Goth tribe. He mouths the name of the tenant who invited him, she shakes her head, can't hear a word.

The word's Mahmoud. Mahmoud invited me. But I know them all. She doesn't care, waves him past her to the river people. River of seething talk, riverrun of heat, turble of music, a congested hallway, party laughter cracking under the dimmed lights. The house chockfull, crammed, apparitions gathered in fours and fives, a throbbing dumb-dumb dumb-dumb beat emitted from the lounge at the back.

Turble as in bubbled turbulence.

Pleased to have invented a new word, Douglas grins back and presses past Gothgirl with his bottle, his smile thinning as he recognises the thumping cheesy melody. Who the fuck put on Abba? What is it with this retro shit?

Party Time

The 1930s house where this party is happening is on a hill, the night is icy, cloudless December, a few stars managing to prick the rooftop lake of light, St Mary's spire lost in the glow over Stoke Newington, a far churn of cloud lacing remotest Chingford, the Edmonton incinerator chimney emptying its pale night filths across the neighbourhood.

Crouch End blues. The Ally Pally a lump of darkness. Elsinore with the lights switched off, just the cautionary glowing bead from the aerial on top to ward off the cop chopper and low-flying Cessnas. And Mount Fuji fractionally visible, a low ghostly cone at the edge of the wastes beyond the North Circular.

This play of ink pools and twinklings makes throbbing Douglas recall the tunnel he passed through earlier that day, King's Cross to Russell Square, the first time since July 7, thinking of what happened as the train picked up speed along the platform.

His reflection in the murky window across the aisle, plural in reality, three or four Douglases staring back at him, outlines overlapping, and then he sees the lights, in the tunnel's blackness, the pair of amber jewels shining from the wall, then gone. In memory of it, he supposes.

Mournful eyes. Lanterns of death.

Gripping his bottle of Jacob's Creek, Douglas is still aiming for the kitchen at the back when he hears his name shouted. Janine is visible through the arch, attentive to what a bald man is saying. Douglas hears his name called again, louder, turns, sees it's Charles. He's brought three male friends who file in past the Goth.

The first is from the cover of the Sergeant Pepper album, a guy with a buttoned-up long military coat, hair flowing down over his shoulders, granny glasses, nose tipped up slightly, a face like a happy short-sighted mole. Douglas didn't realise Peppers still existed, had been reborn. Followed by a red-faced unshaven fatty who looks like a younger version of the current Home Secretary. And a blond genial lightly-accented guy from Toronto. Hi! Hi.

Janine has gone.

Douglas observes, wondering. Two things, basically. Where's she gone? And what does Janine, thirty-two, feel about Douglas, thirty-seven? Since she split with Dave. Since Douglas split with Hazel. Since they both became single once again. Available for fun. They've always been half-friends. And now?

He pushes on between the shoulders and conversations to the dark tiny crowded kitchen. He finds a forest of bottles on the work surface and makes his contribution, takes a polystyrene cup, fills it with red. Once he only drank white, now it's strictly red. Even though it seems to rot his teeth. Or maybe that's just the aftermath of the years he fell in with a bad crowd who drank Martini Bianco and raved about Martin Amis. *Dead Babies* was their Bible. At the last moment Nabokov extended a chubby hand and saved him from the abyss. Then a patch of unemployment and poverty took Doug, if not quite down to the bench in the park and the company of the bearded members of the Dostoevsky appreciation society with their half-litre bottles of meths, to the level fractionally above – British port from Asda and a taste for the verse of Ted Hughes. Horrible, horrible, most horrible...

Doug!

Mahmoud!

It is so good you could come.

Party Time

Mahmoud: charming, polite, a good friend.

I will talk to you later, Douglas.

Mahmoud explains he is getting a drink for someone. Yeah sure. Talk to you later. That suits D. He needs to know where Janine is. Definitely not in the kitchen. Out the back? There's laughter there. Laughter in the dark.

No, not Janine. A bunch of people Doug doesn't know. They ignore him. He turns back and pushes his way through the kitchen again. That fucking Abba shit is on again. Something must be done. Douglas fingers his circular weapon. When the time is right he'll strike...

He drifts into the candlelit lounge of painful, loud music. Two young giantesses are dancing together. Twentyish. One wearing slashed jeans, the other a tight red mini skirt. Thick-legged, massive-breasted, exposing acres of pale skin. One a crop-haired synthetic blonde, the other with a mass of stark black hair shaken across her giant shoulders. Lesbians, Douglas deduces. But showing an agreeably generous amount of cleavage. Their breasts move like manoeuvring zeppelins. Stop staring, Douglas, you filthy pervert! Give the outlandish similes a break, for krissake!

A cleavage, stared at long enough, becomes an arse. Magritte would have understood this. Anyone here in a bowler hat?

I hate Abba almost as much as I hate... Blair, Thatcher, Pinochet, Sharon. A conventional enough list, admittedly. Dangerously conservative. A bit long in the tooth. So very last year...

Then he sees Janine. On the sofa in the far corner, deep in conversation with the bald man. Who Doug doesn't know. The college lecturer type. Bastard. I hate bald men. What do women see in them?

Douglas drains his cup and decides to stride across and demand that she dances with him. Go in with all guns blazing. But even as he drops the cup into a bin he's too late. The bald lizard has read his mind and is helping Janine to her feet. The two of them starting to jive.

Waterloo! Oooh-oooh Waterloo!

Douglas retreats in pain. He fights his way back to the kitchen for a refill. There he encounters Charles. They chat. Great blog, Doug! I read it every day! Fuckin' brilliant man. Makes me laugh...

Doug has a blog called To Be Perfectly Blunt. A mixed bag of daily ravings, some political, some literary. He named it after an expression of his father's. Doug's father is a Tory magistrate. A classic bigot. Which is why Doug rarely goes home to deepest Derbyshire.

So how's things at work?

Charles grins. It slackened off in September. After people had forgotten July. But now we're getting busy again. The build up to Christmas. The three Ps. Pickpockets, piss-heads and punch-ups. Hang on a sec. Hey, you have to smoke in the garden! Or in the street. NOT IN THE HOUSE!

Charles is yelling at three girls who've just been admitted. All fag in hand. Neither Janine nor Charles nor Mahmoud smoke, and the rule is their visitors don't either. And Charles is the enforcer. But then he is a cop. Of sorts. The Met wouldn't have him, so he ended up with the British Transport Police. Fantastic pay. And he'd only been working for six weeks when the bombs went off. Doug was gobsmacked to see Charles on TV on July 8, standing just behind the Commissioner at King's Cross.

And Charles has the story of what really happened

down there. About the remains. Gobbets of human sludge. Barbecued shin bone and roasted hand. The severed head, with eyes that still looked startled. How, in the end, they didn't really need coffins. Shoeboxes would have done. The torsos thinned by fire and high explosive and rats.

The rats! They nosed the feast from miles away, the rats did. They came pouring down the tunnels, whiskers quivering, skipping over the dead rails. Hundreds of them. A squeaking thrilled mob. Changing at King's Cross for the Piccadilly line. A huge rat banquet. Creatures too crazed with vampire hunger to be scared off by the shining of a bright light, or an angry shout, or the fierce kick of a transport policeman's heavy boot.

So they sent in the dogs. Charles is telling the story now. On his way back from escorting the three delinquents to the back garden he pauses to chat up a couple of apparently man-less girls. And there are some girls who really go for cops... And the dogs dealt with the rats, Charles grins. Only problem was – and now Douglas hears one girl shriek and spill red wine down her floral breast, hears the other grimace and say loudly THIS IS GROSS – only problem was the dogs started feasting on what the rats had left...

Abba have been displaced by Van Morrison, a big improvement but still not good enough for Douglas, fingering his secret.

And now a girl is being sick into the metal dustbin outside the back door, is Charles to blame for this? The splatter has an intriguing metallic depth to it. Douglas has always had an artist's appreciation of the depth, richness and sheer variety of human vomit. Turds, too. Tiny, perfectly formed eyeball turds. Bigger, ragged meatballs. And giant sausages from the Tesco Finest range. Then there's dog turds, of course. Somewhere Douglas has a copy of the rare Loudon Wainright B side about the enigma of white dog turds...

Someone fiercely slams the back door shut on this unpleasant interior monologue. Followed by a scraping noise as someone drags the bin to the end of the yard. The girl reappears, wiping her sleeve against her mouth. And attacks a can of Adnams.

Tarkovksy, a Welsh medical student is saying to Douglas (when did this conversation begin? – Douglas has no memory of it ever starting), he's fucking great, man.

Douglas Moog, cooling, assents to this proposition. *Mirror*, it is agreed, is the best of the lot. *Stalker* was weird. *Ivan's Childhood* stunning. The student is freckled, ginger hair, he seems tight. Moog doesn't like the way Ginger casually reaches forward and rests his right hand on Moog's left shoulder. As if to steady himself. But he does not remove it. It makes Moog nervous. If the guy is gay he's picked the wrong man. Moog says: gotta piss, and detaches himself. Me too! chuckles the Welsh medical student, pressing against him as Moog pushes through the crowd. The toilet, thankfully, is vacant. Room for two, whispers the Welshman against the back of Moog's neck. Douglas shuts the door firmly in his face. Perhaps I should feel flattered, he thinks. It must be at least two years since someone tried to pick me up under the delusion I'm gay. That was in his leather jacket and moustache phase.

Outside on the landing the Welshman has gone. There's just Mahmoud, deep in conversation with a beautiful six foot blonde. Plus, naturally, the queue for

Party Time

Howard's sweet shop.

Girls go for sad-eyed delicate Mahmoud. Or rather a certain sort. Six feet tall, slim-to-frail, well educated, usually blonde. Generally from stinking rich families based in Surrey or Hampshire. Often writing Ph.D. theses or archaeologists. For some reason Mahmoud's girlfriends are keen on fantastically expensive leather boots. Douglas wonders if anyone else has spotted this apart from him.

These girls are way outside Douglas's league. Douglas lacks the looks. He's too boringly ordinary. His hair has started to thin. Only a fifty pence piece so far but he knows where that's leading. Another five years and it'll be a saucer, another five a dinner plate. Then there'll be nothing to do but shave off the final rotting shreds and end up looking like one of the stars of *EastEnders*. Mind you, Douglas has always rather liked the way *EastEnders* represents physically unprepossessing men as utterly irresistible to attractive young women, albeit proletarian specimens who, he suspects, would look blank if you were to say: William Burroughs, yer like him, does yer?

These Surrey blondes are drawn to Mahmoud's sadness, his gentleness. He's very polite. Courtly, in a wacky old fashioned way. The sort of person who holds a door open for women. And not just beautiful women; ghastly old hags too. I mean, who the fuck does that these days?

Mahmoud is fabulously good looking. Slim, immaculate, always beautifully turned out. Slightly feminine in the energy he devotes to grooming, appearance, fragrance. But that's not what hooks them. It's the misery. Misery wells out of Mahmoud, he can't help it. The outlet is his eyes. Sad, sad eyes. He looks permanently hurt, forever damaged.

And he is. Mahmoud is from the West Bank. Mahmoud's brother, 23, only has the use of one arm. He was sitting on the balcony of their home reading a book when: crack! An Israeli bullet went through his elbow. For no reason. Just a bored sniper in the IDF watchtower. Keep the smelly Arabs in their place... Plus his cousin lost her baby at a checkpoint. The soldiers wouldn't let her get to a doctor. Keep the Arab numbers down... Things Mahmoud prefers not to talk about it. But he pats Doug on the back and whispers his approval of To Be Perfectly Blunt. Is good you say these things there, my friend...

Mahmoud was invited to speak at the last GMBU annual conference. At a fringe meeting. But then the telephone rang. A man's voice. Very polite. It would be better if you did not speak at this meeting. That was all. No threats. Just a cautionary piece of advice. Velvet-wrapped. So Mahmoud didn't. It turned him to water that they even knew where he lived, that they had his phone number, that they knew all about him speaking to a meeting which, had he spoken at it, would, he knew, turn out to be a large brightly lit room with twelve people spread across the twenty rows, each with twenty plastic chairs.

Douglas would like to know more about Mahmoud's relationships with the blonde fan club but the idea of discussing sex with him is strictly off-limits. Mahmoud is a shy man. Quietly spoken. He would certainly never discuss what went on in his bed. Douglas, were he in Mahmoud's shoes, would get them to remove everything except the boots. Then he'd get them to lie on the bed, face down. And then... Enough of this filth, Moog. You despicable lewd fellow.

Wotcher mate!

It's Howard. Everybody's favourite dealer. Howard has set up shop in the box room above the front door. A queue has formed. Customers line up patiently for what things go better with. Plus other candy. Good to see you, Howard. And you Moog, my man. So what's it to be tonight?

After making his purchase Douglas goes downstairs to see if Janine is still dancing with the despicable hairless one. Encounters her in the crowded hallway down there – people are still pouring in from the street – tall and perfect as she cruises through the crowd, saying gaily to all: I'm going to get my smoke machine.

Doug waves at her. She winks back but doesn't stop. Clad all in leather, creaking as she goes, tight pants shimmering blackly. Her short hair spraypaint scarlet.

Rumour says she doesn't wear a bra or panties, just her leather skin. Douglas swallows hard. A hardness elsewhere, too. He frowns, spotting the baldie bobbing in her wake. As if attached by an underwater cord. Douglas urgently needs another shot of wine. What happened to his cup? Did he leave it in the lav? Can't remember.

In the kitchen is Big Henry, guru of the Progressive Movement for International Workers Democracy – twelve members in all, one quarter blood relations. Operates from a PO Box in Barking. Apt that, thinks Douglas. Big Henry doesn't believe in trades unions. A nutter; a loquacious Stalinist bore. Douglas seizes a new cup, fills it to within a millimetre of its snow-white rim. Gulps down half of it and refills it. Steady, Douglas. Don't get all jacked up. Leastways, not yet.

Beds of roses, Egyptian noses, high pressure hoses –
these are a few of my favourite things.

Eh?

Unbelievable thongs! In Brighton! A nearby girl says.
But this seems very unlikely. Douglas is mishearing, he
must be.

Onion very good for heart attack! Says the girl from
Warsaw brightly. (What girl from Warsaw?)

I feel a little green, says Lettuce, who wishes now she
hadn't had that seventh rum and coke. (But how do you
know that, Douglas? Are you God? That's what Hazel
said. The problem with you Douglas is you think you're
God. Like all men.)

He takes out his notebook purchased in the Louvre
fourteen days earlier and writes:

All the bloodshot mornings, all the dead ends, the
black gleaming highway into the highlands, the sweet
pine forest.

But why did you write that, Moog, my man?

The natives of Lesbos are still dancing, still shaking
their generous flesh. Unperturbed by the amber patterns
which dance on the wall, flaring up like fire.

It IS fire!

Turning, Douglas sees that the man from the Pepper
album is releasing flames from his brain. Fire licks up
out of the top of his head. Roll up, roll up, and see the
human volcano! But Pepperman continues beaming his
vacant hippy stare. Happee hippee. Happee, happee,
happee... And then Sergeant Pepper's grin melts, the
vacancy tightens to bewilderment, expanding.

Charles empties a can of lager over the blaze,

extinguishes what's left with somebody's scarf. He's magnificent. A born emergency worker. Whereas Douglas just gawps stupidly.

Pepperman paws anxiously at the back of his head, sensing his catastrophic loss. A foul stench of burnt hair. Pepperman's own fault, evidently. He backed up against the mantelpiece and its row of candles.

Douglas takes out his notebook again and writes: The sore, the crack whore, and the dead weight of all the American wars.

He has these moments of inspiration. One day they will appear in a piece of fiction. His novel of East End life. Prodigiously influenced by Patrick Hamilton, a disgracefully neglected writer.

That's it, Douglas thinks. This is the absolute bloody limit. More fucking Abba. He snaps. He strides across to the CD player, removes the disk and replaces it with his secret weapon.

Fuck forever!

Go for it, Pete!

FUCK FOR-EVER!

Three cheers for the shambles, folks!

Are these words in his mind being shouted from his mouth? Apparently. People are cheering. Including Janine, who is back with a suitcase. A suitcase? Why the fuck is Janine carrying a suitcase?

She sets it down, opens it, and does some twiddling. And is lost in a surge of smoke. It really is a smoke machine. The sort they use in theatres. Douglas stares, entranced. He never imagined something so relatively small could create an effect like this. Smoke fills the room. It just continues to pour. It's magic. Bugger Harry Potter. This is much better fun!

The lesbians become spectral, then vanish in the smoke. Behind him, in the hallway, the fire alarm starts peeping.

Turn that fucking alarm off!

Mahmoud is on to it. But he's not getting anywhere.

Take the fucking batteries out! THE BATTERIES!

Oh. It's run from the mains. A recent health and safety law, which the spiv landlord has, surprisingly, complied with. So it's impossible to stop without either (i) getting rid of the smoke or (ii) switching the electricity off at the mains and plunging the house into silence and darkness. The second is not an option. Neither is the first.

Peep peep peep peep peep peep peep peep peep peep peep peep peep peep peep peep peep peep peep peep peep peep peep peep peep!

Douglas goes back into the smoke to get away from the monotonous squealing chirp. And collides with the giantess in torn jeans. Her face is spade shaped, powdered, with a violent red lipstick. She smiles lovingly at him, grabs him round the waist. They rock, they roll. Some vile agent of US imperialism has taken the Babyshambles off the machine and replaced them with retro George Harrison.

George fucking Harrison. My Sweet Lord! I really wanna...

Christian shit, in a can of treacle.

She holds him close. Her hot lesbian breath upon his face. Her perfume enfolding him with its violets and gentians. And Janine's smoke boils around them, like they were a couple locked together in Dante's hell. Or death and the maiden. The thin pale wasted man and the pink plump girl.

Party Time

The mystery is how Douglas gets from there to here in the narrative of this night.

From the lounge to the cupboard under the stairs.

Obviously a desperate attempt to flee from the ardent embrace of a lesbian, he decides.

Deep in the warmth of the cupboard under the stairs is not a bad place to be, though. Somehow he's brought a bottle of wine with him. Mystery upon mystery...

Plus there's carpeting! A smell of oil fumes lacing its triangular cave space. Hot pipes emitting a powerful warmth, warm as freshly baked bread. Douglas slips off his shirt, his trousers. Time to sleep...

The chuckling giantess forces him forward, flops across him. How did she get here, this enormous girl? And is it the same girl? Douglas is uncertain. He tastes her sweetly flavoured breath on his lips. She's rippling with friendliness, powdered and delicious. Brimming with sexual enthusiasm. She too is peeling away clothing. Her blouse slips off, exposing a pair of massive breasts. Nipples the size of tangerines!

The pressure of gravity – nothing else but that, your honour – tips him into her embrace.

This big girl may well be an alien, Douglas realises. He has read about these abductions, about what happens. One moment you are taking an invigorating stroll in a lonely pine forest at night, the next you are stark naked and being prodded by a bald entity, after which you are forced to have sex with a lecherous shining creature with very narrow eyes. I was completely helpless, your honour. Overcome by a powerful force.

Outside the cupboard is pandemonium. Smoke pours from the upstairs windows, smoke pours from the open front door.

Smoke, smoke, smoke.

There's shouts in the street, an infinite jest, a kissing hugging laughing crowd on the pavement, where the pillar of cloud rises up toward the other surges, heading for the stars, dispersing thinly in the sodium light.

A neighbour's done the responsible thing, has dialled the three digits, and now here come the consequences. A faraway siren growing louder until it hits the junction, the junction flooded by swimming light, a whirl of urgent blue, the big red engine coming up the hill, men inside still struggling into their carnival costumes, their beaked yellow headgear, the engine braking outside the house, a door already open, a fireman leaping out with axe in hand, another heading for the hoses.

He is too old for this big soft pink girl, Douglas thinks. How old is she? Twenty-two? Big with the depravity and careless fire of the young. Lecherous for meat. Wanting it all, and more. Fancying him, why? Because he seems older? More fucking mature? Or is it a more mature fucking she's after? Someone in less of a hurry than a lusty seventeen year old?

In the cupboard under the stairs, in the smoke filled dark house, Douglas knows at last what he is, knows what the girl is, the two of them.

Astronauts!

Astronauts far away in space, and the great ship falling apart, alarms going off. There's a thumping noise on the wall panels but it can safely be ignored, it's over now. Nothing matters, the losses, the breakages, it's trivial in the face of this enormous doom. It's like the end of *Alien*, it's time to quit and head for home, but the desire for home is gone, he plans to stay. To stay until the end, the final astounding explosive obliteration.

Party Time

Douglas leans into the giantess, putting his tongue to her nipples, plunging his right hand into the moist warmth, playing an old tune. Her eyelids drop down, a tiny smile pulls at the corners of her mouth. A naked film noir bulb shining hotly down over their lust.

No, she says after a while, taking hold of his wrist. Not your finger, your tongue. And gently takes hold of the sides of his head, forcing him down into the jungle, its well of perfume, the mouth of many lips, down to the dripping button. Fumes of desire flow from her like heat. He applies his skills, the slide and curl, sensing the imminence of her delight, the tightening of pleasurable muscle.

Her howl makes the whole house rock. Her pelvis quakes. Some women make the merest whisper. This one's a howler. Douglas's hands lock together at the base of her spine and he hangs on, afraid of being shaken off by the convulsions. When they begin to subside, he rises, kneels a moment, and swiftly enters her. The moment the palms of Janine's hands brush against his pale rear the excitement is too much. He starts ejaculating.

What did you call me, the girl asks. Just now. What did you call me? Her words seem very far away. Considerable energy would be required to respond. He strokes her enormous breasts and says how gorgeous she is. She takes hold of his hair and forces him back down between her thighs. Insatiable.

Time passes. An hour at least. Decades.

It occurs to Douglas that he is a prince trapped in an enchanted castle. Sticky cobwebs bind his upper thighs. Ivy touches his buttocks, his hair. He is nude, in a tub of dark treacle. But pleasantly warm. No, not a prince. Vegetable matter. Anything that lacks a consciousness of self. I know: Fungus!

Fungus has low self-esteem but Douglas has always admired the stuff. It sprouts out of hard, inhospitable wood. It sips nourishment from the merest moist crack. It billows up like pale cloud, delicately speckled. Good enough to eat. It cleverly survives, taken little notice of, provoking at best indifference or revulsion. I am a wedge of pale fungus. I am a honeycomb of delicate rot, a luxuriant parasite lodged against a plump sweating forest torso. I will keep very still. Fungus doesn't talk. I will live forever, becoming as fat and wholesome as my host.

But sleep is not yet permitted him. The hungry giantess is back, lapping around his waist. Lower. She cups his sceptre. Her hot appetite fixes on his now tiny member. Pneumatic lips feast on its apathy. She guzzles its hood. She sups on its solitary teardrop. She swallows its loose, lazy, rubbery stub. Stirs it to fresh action with the to and fro of her wet burning tongue.

Stiffly he agrees to enter into another fleshly transaction. He flops into her ditch. His delay, his slow, rocking, slopping pace suits her fine. She's so slippery he plops out unintentionally, has to take the plunge again.

In deep. He rides her with a measured regularity. After ten minutes she comes. Under the sweltering night sky she roars with enjoyment beneath him. A pleasured cowgirl. He continues to gallop across the featureless plain of their dark intercourse. He feels like he could go on until morning. Minting metaphors and similes under the winter stars. Until the bright dawn gilds her freckles. The booze has given him a strange metallic strength. But she's hot. She's lewd. She's a girl who swaps dirt with her lovers. A dirty, dirty, girl. She's learned the triggers. He feels her forefinger toy with his anus. O Jesus, James Joyce, Janine! Thirty second later and he's shooting his seed into her again.

Blissed out, flesh against flesh, limbs entangled, they drift off across the soft wastes where sleep begins. Idly, Douglas reaches for the power switch above his head and pushes it up. The bulb goes out. There are shouts from somewhere in the house. Someone tries to open the cupboard door, then gives up and goes away.

Total silence, now.

And the word love used not once during the entire performance. Better that way; best to be honest. A fucking good show. A good fucking show. Show good a fucking...

He doesn't even know her name. But he knows it's not Janine.

A dream disease, transmitted by a remote desolate anxiety, begins carelessly to incubate. Down from the guttering it falls, down the window pane it drips. Turns to a translucent worm, wriggling off into the wings. Returns as a slash of blackness, a jittery rushing mouse. Into that narrow gap of grease and hairs under the throbbing fridge. Emerging from the panel of the back door as a mushroom cap. Fast-forward inflated into fungus.

Pricked.

All over, now.

Fungus deflates like a collapsing cheese soufflé. Fungus crumbles like a frail sheet of burnt paper. Fungus drops from a trunk and shatters like china. Douglas turns restlessly, unconscious, grimacing. A quick meaningless stab of pain in the gland of his prick. It doesn't wake him.

The house is mausoleum dead now, no noise at all, except in that corner where clocks and wristwatches shed a shower of rivets. Everyone has gone off down the hill or is sprawled under a duvet. Everyone is drugged, liquor-logged and sodden, fucked or unfucked, every which way asleep.

This night in time will dissolve – but not yet. In the morning there will be a prospect of wreckage. In the morning things will feel sticky and strained. It will be raining. The reckoning will be called for. In the morning there will be conversation, decisions, breakfast. A bowl of shreddies, saturated in milk that doesn't taste or smell quite fresh. Weak tea from a chipped mug. A kettle with a filament encrusted with polluted coral. An icy and growing knowledge of who did what with who this long night. Janine will be there, looking tense and tearful, smoking a cigarette. Having newly given up on her nicotine celibacy. Douglas won't know what to say to her.

But not yet. Not in this hour of darkness. This story is over, the next one hasn't begun. And Christmas – gross, hearty, tinsel-strewn Christmas, big and extravagant as a plum-loaded tumour – hangs over this house like a chandelier of glass tears, about to drop and spread its piercing weight.

THE KISS

As he approaches today's dead children Doodles McMaster closes his lips. His breaststroke forms a small bow wave which makes the dead children bob a little as he meets the first of their motionless bodies. Doodles puffs out his lips, then tightens and thins them. He presses forwards against the carpet of dead children. There are three thousand today, just as there are every day. Today's corpses will join yesterday's three thousand. Tomorrow's will join today's. There is no smell of putrefying flesh. The bodies are too fresh for that. Rigor mortis has set in, as swiftly as it always does, so much faster than you might imagine if you have no experience of the freshly deceased. The faces of the dead children are waxy and yellowish, resembling a fine olive oil. Doodles' eyes twinkle as he glimpses Zoe. At first he could not see her. Zoe is just the other side of the three thousand dead children. She grins at Doodles and waves as he swims closer. The dead children do not upset her. Someone walking on her private beach at low tide upsets her, but the dead children are not a problem. They are there but they cause no real upset. They are quite a long way out and rarely come close. They never wash up on the shore or become entangled with the tasselled legs of the pier. Doodles cuts through the dead children, their bodies bumping against each other as they bob out of his way. Zoe blows him a kiss and Doodles winks back. Now he is through the last of the dead children and moving in towards the shore. Dripping, he runs out of the shallows. Zoe throws her arms around him. Seeing this, the witness shapes what he has seen into words. Doodles kissed married Zoe on a night out. Upper case, bold. The dead children are now so far away there is nothing to see. A faint shadow, a line at best. Most probably imaginary.

CURRENCY EXCHANGE

Damnation! cried Doodles McMaster, thirty-three, exasperated. He was not known for his susurration. Does no one here speak English? *Per me si va nella citta dolente Per me si va nell'etterna dolore*, the sign had said. *Si* meant if and *dolore* meant dollars, but the place looked more like the catacombs of Kiev than a place for the exchange of foreign currency. How clearly he remembered Kiev and the mummified remains and the wide streets and the hordes of lazy locals who had never learned to speak English. Doodles McMaster plunged on down, swearing each time he stumbled on the uneven floor. Shirt, fork, bigger. His jug ears – his friends called him Prince – distorted sound on Tuesdays. Strangely, it was a Wednesday. Damned Italians, he muttered. The dark narrow corridor contained occasional see-through panels which reminded him of the Viking museum. Waxwork dummies with agonized expressions huddled in the imaginary behaviour of long dead societies. Doodles mopped his brow with the noun he always kept in his pocket. He was in good shape for a man his age. The heating was on, even though it was August. Damned, damned Italians. Doodles plunged on down. The special effects were unimpressive, he thought. Perhaps a faint influence of *Aliens*, but without the budget. The flickering of fire against the walls was in fact reminiscent of nothing so much as the crude lighting effect to be seen in his own home in Basildon, in the gas fire with the mock plastic coals. Just as his exasperation reached a new pitch of intensity he was gratified to encounter a figure dressed in a Roman toga. 'Eeengleesh tryst?' the man asked. 'Bujwah?' It took considerable effort to work out that what the fellow meant was 'tourist' and 'bourgeois'. Once the difficulty had been smoothed out the guide helpfully took him off to a place which contained many others like Doodles. It resembled an airport when there's a strike on. Thousands of furious travellers. Some shouted angrily, some wept. Others slumped asleep, their mouths wide open. Doodles attempted to push his way to the front, but was forced back. Someone punched him, but luckily the blow only brushed his shoulder. He was grateful for the dislodged particles of dust. Then, to his lukewarm surprise, a troop of small figures no more than a metre high trooped in. There were wearing devil masks and latex skin suits with tails. The tails reminded Doodles of the time he'd been to see *Cats*. Each devil was carrying a small pitchfork. It seemed dreadfully retro. It was faintly reminiscent of a bad pantomime in a draughty church hall in Penge. He hoped these children weren't going to be allowed to go to the front just because of their age. Also, where were their teachers? Standards were falling again. He might well vote Conservative at the next election if this kind of thing continued. Then the nearest devil stabbed him in the leg. 'Damnation!' cried Doodles. 'That hurt!' The devil did it again. 'Stop that! Stop that at once!' But suddenly the

Currency Exchange

devils seemed to increase in number, and every person there had at least six on them at once. Doodles felt the sharp prongs prick his dainty buttocks. He yelped in fury and pain. His eyes filled with salty liquid distortions. Along with the other pulsating tourists he was driven forwards. From those at the front he heard terrible screams, as if people were falling over the edge of something. This suspicion was confirmed by the way the crowd was rapidly reducing, and by the way those in front just seemed to drop from view. Doodles McMaster decided there must be some mistake. He pulled out his wallet and waved a handful of banknotes in the air. "See! I have many dollars! But I need euros!" he screamed, and went on screaming, until the hot inevitable end.

BLOODY, COLD

Summer was over. September was just about dead, and that day the cold kicked in. Doodles felt it in the early morning darkness when he went for a piss. He'd been in a T-shirt for months, now he dragged on a sweater to meet the day. Cold had gotten into the hollows of his bones, he was talking Tudor, he was whispering to himself. He felt Californian but he knew it wouldn't last.

He didn't bother turning on the light. He heard the Lithuanians go by. He listened to the jet hit the tarn, the crackle. The foamed urine hissed as its honeycomb collapsed. He was not yet fully awake. A part of him was still in St Petersburg, with Theodore. The rest was in the vortex.

Morning was azure, with an edge. The sky burned, it hurt his eyes. The zed in azure had broken free. Loose wire scratched against the echoes inside his head, someone was shaking scraps in there again. He shouted, and the sounds flew away. The noises gathered on the billowing ivy which had attached itself to the back and side of the house. The noises grew feathers, and Doodles wondered if they were sparrows. They looked like sparrows. They were ninety per cent sparrows. Only ten per cent was missing, and that was their dimension. They were too small. Someone was fucking with his mind again. It wasn't Theodore. It was Fyodor.

Doodles made himself a coffee. He was in the kitchen, now. He flicked on the monochrome TV. The headlines showed that the usual straights were out there still, killing, making a killing. Greenland was cracked open, weeping. In seventy years water would be lapping at the ivy. Doodles didn't feel involved. Seventy years was too far away, too hard to imagine. It felt cold, anyway. How could the globe be too hot when he was this cold?

He left the house, and the plates with ketchup smears, and walked off to get his fix. He took the route he knew. The big broken sign was still there, just before the pub. It was a metal sunflower. The glass of the dark greasy sun had been smashed for months. The casing had snapped off at knee height. Rust was feasting on the sign's malnutrition.

In the newsagents he bought a paper from the little Tamil woman. He went on, past the cable TV junction box. The banana skin was still resting on top from the last time he'd passed. Now its stiff curls made it look like a gutted lizard. A row of houses, a community hall, a derelict building. More houses. A car repair yard. An alleyway, a dumped fridge. He walked on, reached the place, knocked on the door. He stood, hearing drums. He waited. The roll-down blind which obscured the glass in the top panel of the door trembled. A pale thin girl with ginger hair stared at him. Mister Wheaty, he mouthed. Two bolts crashed. A lock turned. She opened the door a First Folio's width. He saw the gold chain. I'm Doodles McMaster, he said. Mr Wheaty knows me. She unhooked the chain and let him in. Doodles hadn't seen her before.

She looked younger than Julia. Twenty, maybe. Mr Wheaty had a fondness for freshness. A tip of her head meant: that way.

He didn't need telling. Doodles knew where to go. The second room on the right. Doodles had been here before. He liked Mr Wheaty. He needed Mr Wheaty. Mr Wheaty was famous in those parts. He was reliable. Zina the Greek had recommended him to Doodles. You should go to Mr Wheaty, she said. Doodles trusted her advice. She knew her medicines.

Doodles paid for the two shots. Empurpled notes, naturally. The transaction took place on a street named after a famous Victorian statesman. The outlook was good. Clear skies for a fortnight. The hypo was clean and beautiful. Doodles didn't feel the point of the first one at all. Just the rush. Mr Wheaty was from Tokyo. He seemed faintly androgynous. He had authority but he was gentle. The second syringe hurt, even through the swelling pleasures of the first one's juice it hurt. Mr Wheaty should take more care. He wasn't gentle at all. He was a clumsy Japanese hoodlum. He had a sideline in pirated DVDs.

The rush went with its tides across the ocean, and the lake, and down all the tiny tributaries. Doodles felt its blossom, its swell, its ice and falls. He was on a barge in Kroywen with Alex. He was in St Petersburg, drinking with Theodore. As they finished the vodka the ice on the frozen canal cracked like shots.

Mr Wheaty had style. For Christ's sake, this wasn't a Glaswegian suburb. More of a Buddhist sanctuary. He had Kandinsky on the wall, the oriental. And a big map. Mr Wheaty owned a complete set of Charles Dickens. Their orange spines were heavily wrinkled. He adverted frequently to *Bleak House*. Is that the one with the fog? Doodles wondered. He was a big fog fan. Its infrequency and general depletion perturbed him. He distinctly remembered a faraway day when Chingford was completely invisible.

Doodles giggled. His humour was there for all to see. See! The Kandinsky contains coloured darts! Doodles rested and watched as they took off, flew around the room, returned to base. Sometimes, you know, they are flakes. They drop like autumn leaves around the brass statuette of the Buddha, then vanish at your touch. The map is a map of the world. Play some of the 'Ghost' Trio, some Mississippi Sheiks. The shakes, yes. The room contains a perfect clarity. You cannot help laughing.

Doodles stares at it, the map. His concentration intense. Ginger offers him coffee, but he waves her away. The wildwater raft takes him tumbling on down to the falls. The screams are those of pleasure, of fear inside restraints and adjustments. Hazel is there now, mysteriously. She tightens the belt, cups his scrotum, teases him with the feather, pricks him playfully with the tip of the serrated steak knife. Wraps the scarves around his wrists.

He'd often wondered where Chad was. Chad was at the heart of Africa.

Brazil is enormous. Half of all Latin America is Brazil. Nuts!

Leave my balls alone!

Doodles felt as delicate as that stupid shepherdess on his crazy's aunt's mock marble mantelpiece. He felt as tender as uncooked steak. He felt the vibrations which shimmered from his flesh. They stretched across the road named after the eminent Victorian. They made him think of the ectoplasm weirdness in *Donnie Darko*. He was in the vortex, now. It is in the straits of Sicilia, not far from Aldeburgh. Turn right at the desolate marsh and follow the dull red sunset as far as the muddy pools. You can't miss it.

That sunset, by the way, was the colour of the rust on the piles of Southend pier. And by the way, he knew it would be hard work crossing the road, and it was. The street had the dangerous angles of a Cubist portrait. The swollen corners of parked vans jostled, masking the big-eyed creatures which came at him in silence, on dark wheels. He waited at the cliff of the kerb. He kept his balance. Don't look down. Never look down.

The hours passed. Nothing would keep still. Finally a brown blackbird told him to cross, so he made for the opposite shore. Decaying wharfs formed by the travel agency, but they were gone in a blink. Magic.

Moon high in the sky, he zag-zigged homeward. Bright as a yolk. A high bright image turning in his vision, of something that cracked apart in flakes of Kandinsky, then flew back toward the void, and filled it, and became whole again. He ziggy-zooged homeward.

Mr Wheaty said: Looking for a tasty way to whole grain goodness? Mr Wheaty called out: People with healthy hearts eat more whole grain food as part of their healthy lifestyles! Mr Wheaty slipped in a little pantothenic acid, all to make Doodles McMaster as wholesome as wholesome can be. Thank you, Mr Wheaty!

Top banana!

He felt damned good. It could not be denied, he was having one hell of a time!

Under a bitter moon the dead lizard moved. The dead

lizard moved, he could have sworn. Maybe the junction box was responsible. It had the rough texture of a crocodile's skin. The dull greenish colouring, too. He realised now that the junction box was a crocodile which had cunningly folded itself up and was waiting to strike, just like in the wildlife documentaries. Things did not look good for that herd of gazelles making the great migration south from Stoke Newington. Junction boxes can move at extraordinary speeds when they want to, he knew that for a cast iron truth.

The zebra crossing had become the keys of a giant piano. As he walked across it the pressure of his trainers forced deaf, sullen Beethoven to play. It was a simple, pleasing melody. 'Für Elise', he wouldn't be at all surprised. Which is Lithuanian and means: for Ellis.

Doodles seemed to be walking downhill. He had never noticed the slope before. Until this day the whole world had been flat. Now he was gathering speed. Perhaps the thaw in Greenland was having a greater impact than oceanologists realised.

It is a little know fact that the word *Charybdis* occurs only once in Shakespeare. Miching mallecho! And George Jones's favourite record is Tammy Wynette's 'Take Me To Your World'. And in the summer of 1790, in Ipswich, a middle-aged poet named George Crabbe was seen suddenly to stagger and fall. He was thought to be drunk. A calumny! And in the autumn of 2005, in Greater London, Doodles McMaster was seen to halt in the street and look afraid. He had just seen the police car up ahead. It was parked at the side of the road. His side. Doodles realised he was sweating, he was terrified. Cops did that to him. They triggered memories.

The steepness of the slope forced him towards the

white terrible vehicle. Rounding a curve he realised there were two cops there, standing at the back of the footway, obscured by an overgrown bush. They were waiting for him. They knew all about him. It was an ambush. Doodles knew they would ask him to stop, and then start talking to him. Bellicose and scowling and burning with suspicion. They knew his sort. He knew their sort. And Doodles knew he had nothing to say. Not today. Today he wasn't talking. Not even to Hazel. If they asked him any questions he would just shake his head. He wasn't going to tell them about the lizard or the crocodile or the woman who tried the locked door and went away. Her skin was olive, she was small, that was all he remembered. She was from the first draft. She'd been deleted. And he certainly wasn't going to tell them about Hazel.

As he drew closer he saw that the cops were standing either side of a blonde woman, who was sitting on a low brick wall.

They'd got Hazel!

No, not Hazel. Hazel was younger. This woman looked to be in her thirties. Her long hair touched her shoulders. She looked smart, she wasn't a tramp. But her face seemed faintly florid, with a marbling of fine eggshell blue veins. Her cheeks were reminiscent of those of Brad Pitt in *Interview with the Vampire*. Doodles wondered what she was. A whore, a crack addict, a vampire? There was trouble here.

I'm shivering. I'm cold. I want to sit in the car.

That's what the woman said as he passed, and the white cop said, You just stay there. Just wait. The white cop had a thin flat head shaped like a playing card. His blackhead-studded fat fluffy nose was an ace of spades.

58

Bloody, Cold

The ambulance will be here soon, he said. Or perhaps: The van will be here soon. Doodles didn't catch that second word. The Asian cop said nothing. He stood there, alert, like the vampire might try to flee.

Doodles dragged his toxic condition and his shimmering tentacles of ectoplasm past the cops and they didn't even notice. Cops are stupid. Cops are the garbage men of the capitalist state. Cops are always young, with cruel eyes. They cut their hair short because of the lice. Their fists are hairy and hard.

Doodles left them behind. He was leaving everything behind, he could feel it. Even those tiny mysterious drips of blood from the blonde's brimming left ear. The angle of the neighbourhood had distinctly changed. Now he was toiling uphill. Thirty degrees became forty-five. Now Doodles was breathing heavily and making little grunts. His armpits were giving birth to hot wet worms. The worms melted into the fabric of his black T-shirt. The black T-shirt whispered something he couldn't catch. He turned his head slightly at the prospect of two workmen. They were carrying a sheet of glass, like in a Hollywood comedy. It glittered with foolish snakes. Only the mildest adjustment was all it took to shake the reptiles off. The glitter dropped to the ground, frothing simultaneously. An evaporation completed the performance. Doodles briefly examined the ash marks. The message was in morse; he could never decipher it.

Doodles went on. The sky was azure, with a silver blade. The birds were big and dark and went over low, hundreds of them, honking. Their shadows touched him and toyed with him like big fast gentle death. A siren whined a long way away. He felt its silver, its chill. It was coming to collect his corpse. By the time it reached this hill he would be stiff and cold. He decided not to stay for it. Another time, another place. He had a hundred and one damnations to attend to first. They must not be neglected. They each depended on him for nourishment.

Doodles was getting near the summit now. The rush carried him on. He ran up the scree, hand in hand with Hazel. Her laughter was smooth, like velvet. Her breasts had a saddle of dimples. She was an easy, adventurous girl. Libidinous, fond of Irish coffee. Twenty-six. She liked her fix and gave good licks. Her father was an alcoholic. She was not one to be in bed by eleven, unless there was the promise of good meat. On Sunday mornings they lay in bed listening to The Christians, a group whose popularity is fading. The God squad gathered across the street in their best clothes to sing hymns alongside a thumped, joyous piano. There is a green hole faraway. Onward crisp tin soul jars. All thongs tight and wonderful. Sometimes you could hear the preacherman, the boom and echo of his low excitement. The shine in his eyes bored holes in the buttresses. Out of them shot his dullard's hard narrow ringing certainties.

The spire pressed its sharp point against the sky, held by the calm of Mr Wheaty's gigantic hairless hand. The view across the Himalayas was lovely. The incinerator chimney looked very elegant against the cloudless sky. No smoke today. It occurred to Doodles that Mr Wheaty was in tune with eternity. That was an insight you'd never find inside a cracker.

On the top of Everest there is little space to move. You have to brace yourself against the draught, legs far apart. The air is bitter and thin and biting. The leather of your lungs goes hard up there, and it hurts. Doodles withdrew the magical device from his survival outfit. It wasn't easy, what with the blizzard, the darkness of his snow goggles, having to use mittens.

He managed to get the jittery key into the wriggly lock. He opened the door to the darkness. He went inside. Another vibrating achievement for Doodles McMaster!

Welcome to Chad. Chad is a small, cold country. The ice there is melting. Chad is entirely covered by carpet. Doodles noticed that the carpet was blood red. He lay down on it. He listened to the drip-drip of water. It reminded him of something. Of two things. A movie. A poem. The movie ended with a Four Tops song, the poem ended in what's shored.

Shore thing, pardner!

Eh?

Is that you Tom, Franz?

Hazel?

Memphis blues.

The ivy started crawling towards Chad but Doodles didn't mind. He had all day ahead of him, and all the long night too. He was expecting a long night. He'd lined up the tabs, the bottles, the mugs. He had other equipment waiting too. He had two John Travolta movies to take his mind off what was going on, and what was going on was the cold, and the thaw, and the coming winter, and all the confusion, which is an interesting word. It has fusion inside it. And a fuse. Doodles lit a match and tried to light it but the flame went out.

Now it is very dark and very cold and when I piss into the bowl I see blood. I haven't seen it like that in a long, long while. Not since my days in Greenland. And now I am in the East End, which is called that because that's where you end up when you go west. No, that can't be right. Because it is where people go who have reached the end. The East End is full of ends, and odds, and endings. Especially odds. And the occasional dead lizard. And concealed alligators. And now the ivy is lapping at my feet and winding its way around my ankles. I kick it away. I should go start the Travolta movie. But I don't.

It is time for a beginning. October is a good month for this. It is the coldest month because I remember the October dead. There are so many of them. Seven is a magic number, did you know? Seven pillars, seven ambiguities. Magnificent! I can't catch flies the way I used to, so fetch me some black gloves. I must wear black gloves. Funeral gloves. So much death, so much blood. And the cold, getting colder all the time. So cold I withdraw my fingers from the keyboard. I slip away and sink. The keyboard bobs and drifts away in the dark.

I lie on the worn carpet, which is blood red, with white criss-cross patches where the pile has gone. Now I'm drinking red wine and my hand is shaking. I'm dribbling, I'm spilling it down my sweater. What a bloody mess! Bobok, I say, just for a laugh. Bobok.

The wine tastes salty, like blood. Summer is definitely over. I stare at the previous sentence for a long while, until the screensaver cuts in. It's on a customised seven minute setting.

So cold, so very cold.

A cube with red and green sides explodes.

The fragments drift in space, merge, and become a cube again.

And so it goes on.

DIRT ENTERS AT THE HEART

It was the year your favourite author was Saul Bellow, your drug was cannabis, your dealer was Alain, your girlfriend's name had four syllables. You dabbled, eight of you, in black magic. There were markings on the floor in a derelict building you accessed by a dry drain. Sarah said it reminded her of *The Third Man*, a movie you had yet to see. George was the driving force behind the occultism. He'd spent his adolescence consuming the fiction of Dennis Wheatley. He was seriously disturbed. It was all just an excuse for sex, really. That and drug taking. The atmosphere was smoky. Someone brought along some skulls, real ones. Alain was into Enya and the Incredible String Band. In winter the rain beat down on the corrugated roof of the abandoned building. The bright cheeks of Alain and George testified to the abuse they put their bodies through. The girls were just along for the fun of it. They were from places like Bath and Cheltenham and Saffron Walden. The affluent parts. Their daddies were diplomats and bankers. Belinda's was a stockbroker. Everyone needs a little depravity before they tumble into a career. The eight of you hunkered down in the smoke and called up Satan. None of you expected him to show. There was a warning, first. You would have to live with the consequences. But you wanted to learn what the future would bring, and you all agreed. You each pricked your arms with a knife and mingled your blood. Amid the smoke you felt Satan's hot breath. He whispered the price that each of you would pay. No real sleep. And Belinda learned the year of her death. It would occur in 2006. At the time it seemed far in the future. Nothing to worry about. Four syllables went from your life not long after. You lost touch with all the others. Alain had a breakdown and found God. He became impossible to talk to. As for the others. The relationships cracked, one by one. Belinda dumped Mick and married a lawyer. She did not invite you to her wedding. Four syllables was last heard of living with a bearded sculptor. George dropped completely out of sight. The derelict site was bulldozed, developed. Houses are there now. Lawns, drives, garden sculpture. And now, sleepless, you lie in bed at four in the morning. You can hear the rain. In the morning, on the train, you read *Herzog* for the first time since those days. But you can't concentrate. You keep thinking of Belinda. You wonder which day. It's March. It may already have happened. You have no way of finding out. You can't even remember her married name. You never knew her birthday. She's impossible to trace. But by the first day of next January she'll be gone. Of that you are certain. It was no trick, in that big desolate room. You can still smell that breath, scented with fire and excrement. You can still hear that husky, hoarse voice, which spoke from no direction. More inside your head than in your ears. And yet the others heard it too. That was the odd thing. Every one of us heard it, not just me.

COMING THAT WAY

I decided to come that way, though it's a sinister narrow road which runs between the backs of two other roads. At the end of their gardens they have garages, and these garages face on to Cut-Throat Lane. Cheery name.

The garages have been put up at different times and many are in a ramshackle, decrepit condition. Two or three are smashed and empty. The lane is popular with graffiti artists.

Occasionally there's a huddle of hooded youths, who gather in the shadows of one of the derelict garages. Sometimes there's a whiff of cannabis.

As I turned in that night I saw two men, standing alongside the small brick wall at the Vaughan Road end. They had four cans of beer lined up along the wall and were smoking cigarettes and talking in an East European language. They at once made me think of my mother.

My mother, on the rare occasions she came to London to visit me, used regularly to say in a loud voice: You'd think you were living in bloody Pakistan!

She had never, needless to say, ventured outside the Bournemouth-Brighton-Birmingham triangle in the entire course of her life, which was terminated by lung cancer at the age of seventy-three. Her *Weltanschauung* was exclusively shaped by the contents and editorials of the *Daily Express*. Now, I think, she would have been more inclined to say: You'd think you were living in bloody Russia!

Yes, the men were probably Poles – or perhaps Lithuanians. As I drew near the bar I saw an elderly black woman approaching from the opposite side. She scowled at the men as she passed them, and kept her scowl alive as she came closer to me. I could imagine her in an evangelical church, tight and wobbly as jelly, her eyes bright with joy at the connection she was making, via a tambourine, with her powerful shining imaginary entity.

The East Europeans ignored first her and then me. I realised that they had made the little brick wall their beer cellar and that that short stretch of footway was their home. Far from their native land, they were drinking and smoking and talking, in a little space of private warmth. I passed them with a small smile which they were too engrossed in conversation and good cheer to notice.

I hurried on past the garages, meeting no one else. It was a cold night, overcast and gloomy.

As I walked on I suddenly thought of the lost world of typewriters. An entire culture vanished almost overnight! The two sheets of foolscap paper enclosing a sheet of blue carbon paper. The winding in of this sandwich into the machine. The rise of the ribbon as the keys swished forwards and thudded against the paper. The clatter and crack of fast typing.

And then a car drew into the last available space on Shakespeare Crescent. Its headlights dazzled me, and the driver, the bastard, made no attempt to dip them as he manoeuvred into the parking bay.

Coming That Way

I went past the last garage, turned off down Herbert Road, out of the painful scrutiny of the headlamps. Here there was a house with the curtains not yet drawn. A gigantic flatscreen TV flickered with images of a famous newsreader.

I thought: a television is a box containing some of the most beautiful people in the world. Hair, complexion, smoothness of skin, teeth – the magnificence is luminous.

The contrast with those outside this magic box is acute. Me, for example. I am entirely toothless, bald and purple. Small children sometimes point at me in the street and shout: It's mister tomato face! Or that fat woman with the buggy I saw in the supermarket this morning, for example. Her yellow dappled skin unpleasant to consider, her overlapping chins redolent of a poor diet and lack of self-restraint. That fat woman would never manage to squeeze into this dazzling frame. Nor would a frowning evangelical, or two intense East Europeans drinking beside a wall.

But the language of television people is corrupt. Their mouths release lie after shining lie. And I pictured those lies slithering out of every television in this gigantic city, to be captured by tall metal stalks, which suck all the lies up and convert them into electricity, lighting the streets. I wondered if I was going mad, as the priest had warned would happen when he gave me his little green booklet on the dreadful consequences of self-abuse. The eyes of the new Pope certainly seemed to indicate an acute, penetrating understanding of this sticky subject.

I walked on, a little feverish, my thoughts switching to a bottle of red wine, 2003, a good Australian year; to Mayakovsky's assertion that without a rhyme, poetry falls to pieces; to the rat that lives on this street and can sometimes, at dusk, be seen scampering along the gutter, sniffing at rain-configured sludge; to a famous writer and critic, whose fame was already diminished and who, dead, was becoming more depleted, more irrelevant, with each passing year; to the pleasure in splitting open a poached egg on toast; to a bookshop in Camden, long since closed, not all that far from the loft once inhabited by Rimbaud and Verlaine.

As I did so, the clouds thawed, opening up a vista of remote, burning gases. And then I was home, toiling up the cold communal stairwell. Home sweet home! My little garret below a waste of ancient stars! I hummed an old number one hit as I opened the blue door, crossed a hallway, and hurried into a small room with a frosted glass skylight and a toilet duck. Afterwards, the kitchen, and the wall heater with its flickering tiny flame. The poky lounge was buried in its usual clutter of second hand paperbacks. And last of all the bedroom where, rigid and patient, lay my mute, open-mouthed, inflatable sex doll, Jane. The beauty spot on her rump I had put there myself, when a rough love romp had resulted in a need for surgery using the rubber patch from my bicycle puncture repair outfit. Darling Jane! Over the years, a good sport, eager and game for anything, she has granted me infinitely more satisfaction than my brief, unsatisfactory liaisons with Rosa or Juliet ever did.

I poured myself half a pint of red wine and went and sat on the edge of the bed. There I wondered, not for the first time, what it was on the ceiling that Jane was staring at.

THE PHOTOGRAPH

Turning the page and seeing for the first time in Klaus Wagenbach's handsomely illustrated monograph on Kafka the black and white photograph of Julie Wohryzek, the writer's second fiancée, I received a considerable shock. For I realised at once that I had met Miss Wohryzek. Although the circumstances are now a little cloudy – I recall vividly a cold, unfurnished room in a large student residence, on a campus with a lake and some squawking ducks – I remember quite distinctly her eyes and the gist of our conversation.

I was with my then girlfriend, whose identity is now also unclear, because that year I had two girlfriends and after this bleak and troubling passage of time their identities have blurred. It may have been Rosa who was with me. She was a student of physics, tiny and pale and timid, except in bed. Rosa, whose appetite for men was inexhaustible. Or it might equally have been Juliet, who did drama. Her breasts were big as watermelons. I still remember fondly her huge rubbery nipples, which I used to lick until they hardened into granite, reminding me of a favourite location on Dartmoor. Juliet was sensuous and loud, and fond of the Rolling Stones. Miss Wohryzek was a friend of either Rosa or Juliet, and had joined us at the local cinema to see a film.

I no longer remember the name of the film but the plot centred on a man who may or may not have been what he purported to be. There were those who believed his story, and those who disbelieved it. There was the strong suggestion that trickery, insincerity and delusion were jostling for supremacy. The man's situation and the reactions to it of those around him were represented in a satirical fashion which poked fun at various figures of authority – the police chief, the magistrate, the doctor. It was a continental movie, with subtitles. The credits at the end of the movie unrolled over a sequence of tinted landscape photographs which evoked a long vanished world. The unusual colouration greatly resembled some of the photographs of the ancient kingdom of Bohemia in Wagenbach's book – a farm house in Zürau, the old Èech-Bridge with its tramlines and pair of enormous columns supporting winged figures, the hotel in Spindelmülle in which Kafka wrote the first parts of *The Castle*.

After the film we returned to the campus. The room did not belong to Rosa or Juliet, so it seems likely it was Miss Wohryzek's. I had not really noticed much about her until now, since she had met us in the foyer and after the film we returned in darkness. In the harsh light of that room I saw that she kept her hair fastened back in an austere, controlling manner; that she had delicate features, a little marred by her thin, disapproving lips; that she kept her small hands on her lap, as if ready to fend off an impudent assault on her sensible skirt.

It was her eyes that struck me the most. They were hazel brown and full of anxiety and nervousness. I

The Photograph

sensed her disapproval of me. We discussed the film. I was full of enthusiasm for it. I had enjoyed the unresolved ambiguity of the protagonist's identity. The blundering efforts of the police chief, the magistrate and the doctor made me laugh. The director had evidently set out to mock bourgeois society and to challenge its values. Miss Wohryzek disagreed fiercely. She said she had not enjoyed the film. There was nothing in it that made her want to laugh. It was throughout negative in orientation. She disapproved strongly of negative art.

Soon afterwards my spectral girlfriend and I evaporated into air, into thin air. I remember vividly that there was nothing to drink in that room, and the absence of alcohol during an evening has always produced in me severe and distressing palpitations. Probably – almost definitely – there can really be no question about this at all – we went to the nearest bar. I am quite sure that Miss Wohryzek did not accompany us. I am equally certain that I never saw her again.

RIDICULOUS

1

He stood motionless before the cash machine by the supermarket entrance. While he waited for the device to digest the feed he'd placed in its tight little mouth he wondered if it was really true that the Americans had constructed a hypersonic jet capable of travelling at 8,000mph. The contrail in the photograph looked very impressive, but could you trust a television documentary? It wasn't all that long ago that he'd seen a bald Frenchman in a white trench coat solemnly describing the gigantic flash which had been triggered in the underpass, blinding the driver of Diana's car. The Frenchman had subsequently been exposed as a notorious confidence trickster and petty Parisian criminal.

A peep-peeping indicated that the platinum Visa card of D. Elijah McMaster had been half vomited back to him. He plucked it from the slit. His father had not foreseen this strange echoing consequence when he'd pushed his penis inside warm powdered Ellen McMaster and duly ejaculated. Doodles reached down for his three

Ridiculous

bank notes and then the receipt. He blamed his mother for his conception and his father for the preposterous name. Doodles had just put these items away in his leather wallet when the convulsion occurred.

At first he assumed the shadows were inside his vision, which these days was increasingly prone to the flutterings and quick neurotic to-ings and fro-ings of moths, tightrope-scurrying spiders and a solitary bat. The noise – a heavy, obscure clattering punctuated by skiddings and a bellow – was no different to the hubbub which conventionally assaulted him when other noises ceased. But abruptly the convulsion became tangible, enveloped in the cheap but soothingly familiar cloth of realism.

The big plate glass automated twin doors of the supermarket opened and a man tumbled out.

His contours were raggedy and fast-moving, his movements not those of a calm vertical departing customer but a half-running stagger. No, not one man, two. As the first man broke out of the exit, he dragged an appendage, a big shaky balloon of darkness. The second man had hold of the first man's belt. His belt must have been made of elastic. It extended back half a metre to the chubby fist of the second man. Striped yellow, green and black, the attenuated belt looked to Doodles (who had a weakness for early morning similes with his whisky) like a colourful intestine torn from the guts of a martyred heretic.

Both men, Doodles saw, were black. The first man's blackness was of a depth and purity he associated with North Africans, an impression reinforced by a side glimpse of fine features, carved cheekbones, spinning big white eyes. He was skinny. His shaggy ebony-black hair was bound into dreadlocks There was a delicacy about the man, his balance that of a ballerina, he seemed about to fall, but didn't. His trainers dragged and skidded on the gum-dappled flagstones.

The second black was Afro-Caribbean, fleshy and huge, shaven-headed and rippling. His chin and cheeks and chest seemed to flop and change shape in a single tidal motion, the heavy oil of his skin rising to a powerful submarine surge. He had a bouncer's bulk. As the surge boiled through his upper torso this second man bellowed like a bull. A bull's bellow is a cry drawn from the stomach of a gigantic fury – Doodles had once witnessed six men with prods trying to force one up the slatted metal ramp of a car ferry – and it cowed the North African, who went slack. But only momentarily. It was a dancer's feint, he jerked away and got loose from his heavy greedy appendage. His dreadlocks spread like a suddenly opened paper fan.

The twin doors stayed open and a third figure shot out of the exit. He was white, white shirted, black shiny shoed, pink cheeked, gasping, agitated. He stumbled to a stop, hands clamping his waist, bowed over, taking deep loud breaths.

The North African had his hand on the mottled silver handle of the black wooden door to the car park. But the bull, bellowing a second time, had charged. The bouncer was an amoeba with restless shapeless limbs, expanding and contracting. A ball of dark movement. He did not so much seize the North African as envelop him. As the two figures embraced by the still unopened door the white man ran forward and hugged them both. Inside, he said. Let's go inside.

He meant the supermarket, Doodles realised, not the

stairwell to the car park. But the North African had a separate ambition. He attempted to duck down, wriggling, to elude the amoeba. But the grip holding him was fixed and firm. The African's brown woollen jumper stretched but did not fly off and release him into the freedom of a cool October London morning, so he bobbed up again and slid a skinny leg behind the white man's conformist grey cotton trousers. The white man found himself lying on cold hard concrete, with a spreading pain in his shoulder. Bastard, he said.

The two black men now grunted and pushed and struggled like some kind of ungainly four legged clothed creature experiencing the first stabbings of a cardiac arrest. Tottering and rocking, they seemed always about to fall. They skittered backwards and forwards across their tiny arena of gladiatorial combat, attracting a small audience of interested onlookers. Groaning and sweating, locked as one, they might have been lovers engrossed in a rough biting scratching dirty-mouthed coupling, flesh against flesh, lip against cheek, wet and sticky with effort and endurance, drawing blood, knowing the end would be good, would be hotly exciting, goldenly intense. The African yearned for the car park door, but the amoeba was slowly sucking him towards the still open exit doors, where the white man waited, hands on hips, a little bowed, the pressing look of an acute steely constipation on his face.

The North African's ardour seemed to puncture. This time it wasn't a trick. He gave up the fight. Suddenly he was meek, obedient. A surrendered prisoner. His energy had drained off, leaving him slack and weak. Inside, said the white man, his eyes hard and angry. Back into the store went the North African, arm in arm with the security guard. He glided past the cigarette counter, weightless as a sheet of paper. The crowd dispersed; the incident was over.

A shoplifter, Doodles assumed. He went inside and through Fresh Vegetables to buy a slab of Cathedral City cheese, a carton of half fat milk, a 'harvest grain' loaf and a bottle of white wine, a 50/50 blend of Viognier and Marsanne, named after an ancient tower belonging to the provost of Orange, he read on the label, which had a tear along its Atlantic coast.

Apart from the familiar bat, which leapt out from the canned plums at the very edge of his vision and then fluttered away behind the self-raising flour, the rest of his visit to the supermarket that long October day was without incident. At the checkout there was no sign of the men involved in the commotion at the entrance five minutes earlier. The store was as tranquil and orderly as the cemetery at Delville Wood.

2

Rain drums on the corrugated porch outside the kitchen. There's a regular tapping where water drips at four second intervals on to the dustbin's metal lid. Rain splashes and bursts across the concrete patio. It seems to be DARK all the time: a line he always liked. Inside the kitchen the Damien Rice album is playing. Track three makes Douglas think of the DVD he watched at the weekend. Like Kafka on 7 January 1913, he feels chilled through and through.

He removes the wholemeal loaf from its cellophane wrapping. He lays it on the wooden bread board and cuts off the crust at the end. Next he saws off two slices, sending a tiny shower of malted wheat flakes across the formica surface. He butters the slices and arranges some layers of rubbery gruyere on the first slice of bread. He spoons some chutney across the second slice, then presses the two slices together.

Now he leaves the sandwich on the bread board and goes to a cupboard. A close-up shows a tightly packed forest of bottles. At the front is a bottle of wine, with a blue plastic stopper in the neck. Douglas lifts out the bottle and places it on the work surface. He takes down a wine glass from another cupboard, and fills it. Australian red, Cabernet Sauvignon, 2003, a good year that was. He drinks half the glass and feels his hunger quicken. Putting the glass down, he moves over to the bread board. He is reaching down for the sandwich when he sees the hair.

The hair protrudes from the heart of the sandwich. It is barely two centimetres long and dark brown, almost ruddy. A curiously thick hair which, even as Douglas watches, moves. It extends itself and slips a little further from its nest of cheese and butter. Next it pauses, hesitant, at the bread board's edge. Not hair but a worm. A wireworm, in fact.

It releases its full length from the sandwich and wriggles quickly over the edge of the bread board. Now it is making for the wall. A good seven centimetres of it. Replete, no doubt, and now brimming with blood and energy. Disgusted, Douglas grabs at the kitchen roll beside the bread bin, tears off two sheets, and bundles the worm into the tissue. He folds the tissue up, flattens it, squeezes it inside his fist. He's squashed it to a dark dirty smear, surely, but he doesn't open it to check.

Instead he takes it and drops it into the toilet bowl. He watches the tissue loosen and begin to unfold. Unzipping, he pisses hard on the pale sunken wreckage, watching it turn yellow, then quickly flushing, waiting to see if the creature has survived, as sometimes happens with flies or ants, but no, the surface is clear as a swimming pool, the bowl's crystal depths pure and free of any speck of darkness.

Slightly dizzy, Douglas returns to the kitchen, accompanied by an army of dead flies and ants. Risen from their passage through purgatory, they form up into furious columns at the edge of his field of vision, scrappy and prickly, pointing accusing sticks, bits of broken wing. A blink rids him of their boiling presence.

He considers his sandwich. Inside it looks as tasty as ever. The worm can surely not have been in the cheese, which, though full of holes, is smooth and yellow and sealed in cellophane (and besides, is from Switzerland, a land of snow and hygiene and immaculate scented bankers). The spotless slab of butter is equally free of suspicion. The 'harvest grain' loaf? That seems very possible, though the worm would have had to get in between the baking and the wrapping (for the bread, too, has enjoyed the protection of a membrane of cellophane). What about the chutney? Douglas unscrews the lid and looks inside the jar. Its murky, clogged depths seem a likely enough nest for a thriving family of wireworms.

There is no obvious trace of the worm left in the sandwich. But Douglas has now lost his appetite. He throws the sandwich in the pedal bin, and then the loaf, and then the jar of chutney. He finishes the wine and pours himself a second glass. He removes the white sack

Ridiculous

from the bin, knots the neck, and takes it outside. He drops it in the dustbin. The memory of that worm will wriggle around the kitchen for days to come. He replaces the dustbin lid. Rain smashes him with big raw generous dollops of its indifference to a man having a bad day.

3

I am writing to you from the eastern end of things. My routines have not changed greatly since you – and then a hyphen slams the sentence shut.

A month ago, outside the British Museum, I started trembling uncontrollably. I began, uncharacteristically, to cry. A scrap of torn green leaf lay on the third step. Its veins were bruised by the passage of all those who had walked upon it. Passages! Time passages, and that singer in the old church hall, whose guitar string snapped in two. I was with a girl who later became a chartered accountant, whose hand let go of mine, and she was gone. I can still hear the twang of that broken string. I can still see her, but not as vividly as – and then a storm of asterisks.

I have tried to write down all that I remember. The bay, the islands, the direction we were going in. That fire in your delight, the hinge of your replies, these are what I recall most intensely. Not paragraphs. The paragraphs are rotted. Our long conversations, which continued all the way up that coast of rock, are washed away. They are lost in the grey between the wet black pebbles and all those slender uninhabited fixtures. They are bones turned to powder on the bed of the tarns. They are tucked under the moss of all the writers' gravestones I made you attend. A stench of weed rises from our romantic coast and its extraordinary rainbows.

The Lithuanian girl next door told me her mother said talking is bad for you. Too much of it and you damage your lips. This is true, I said. Hush now. You must not hurt your mouth. Preserve your strength, my little one. Preserve it for the time of whispers.

The time of whispers and bones. All ends the same. A departed lover. A friend. A parent. Imperial Caesar. Won't make old bones, my mother said. And chuckled. And died. Across the river and into the black mud. Everything is much smaller when you are older. She faded in her green armchair. She left her sack of loose lined skin behind her like a snake.

The islands were the colour of cigarette smoke. In the bay you called me 'Mr Hendrix', I have never quite understood why. Later you read my stories about Doodles McMaster. Why do you call yourself Doodles, Douglas? Is it the 'D'? Don't call me Douglas, I said. I'm Doodles now. You're weird, Douglas Moog, said she.

I wrote: I have located the therapies of all the lost ones. I have scattered question marks like the confetti I threw at your second wedding. Ardently I copied down the words 'thick tree shadows' and 'quiet voice piling up in mid-air'. You told me I was drinking too much. In Disdain's prison desperate I lie, I said. I doubt that, Douglas, she retorted edgily. Will your rigour never abate? I hurled. By way of reply you put on 'Gallons of Rubbing Alcohol Flow through the Strip'. Your sense of humour was Glaswegian. I particularly appreciated that.

It is a good time of the year for collecting leaves. On the heath I found a spectacularly coloured one – cadmium yellow at the edges, then a band of coral, giving way to rust and a strange coppery brown. You taught me all I know about colour, but that knowledge does not add lustre to – the ending here is deleted. A thousand discoloured veins ran on. Clogged by death. Overwhelmed by rotting adjectives.

On my latest visit to the city centre, this last Saturday, I did not think of you at all. In my imaginary life you still share my enthusiasm for Jean Genet, Blaise Cendrars, Gassan Kanafani. We hurry, arm in arm, across the Millennium Bridge, in pursuit of that novel in which one narrator is a clock, another is a desert. The bridge is deserted and, strangely, leads to the beach at Holkham. It is deserted, apart from a solitary dog walker and her engorged mongrel. The bronzed sands are sculpted into tiny curving ridges and wrinkles. A contrail bisects the blue sky. The sea is faraway, barely visible. And then –

I have continued to search for – and there the sentence faded out. I shall always remember with affection your kindness to the bat. How it loved to settle in the palm of your calm small hand, squeaking and shivering and fluttering its tiny fur umbrella wings as it fed on the worms and beetles you'd gathered up from the pungent putrefaction of the overgrown yard. But in recent weeks I have even begun to wonder what – and then that sentence also ends.

I wake, in great pain, at two forty-five. Half way down my calf the vein feels blocked, frozen, congested. When I touch it I am shocked how hard it feels, as if a stone is lodged just below the skin. Cramp, surely. Just cramp. I raise my left leg and shake it in the darkness, and chop at and massage the lump. I picture the lump as a ball of greasy semi-colons, congealed and stiff as knotted, half-boiled noodles. I described these sufferings to my attractive Eurasian guru. She told me I should imagine I am holding a gigantic wooden spoon and beat myself repeatedly with it. Sound advice! Afterwards I relaxed to a tape of hammered Tibetan bowls. And then a whisky, a whisky, and another sleepless night.

I roll out of bed and limp to the bathroom. I feel sick and old and alone. The pain is less now but there is a numbness in the leg, a stiffness. My doctor said this is how pregnant women get. But I am not a pregnant woman, I remarked. The doctor tipped his bifocals and scrutinised me afresh. That is true, he conceded.

In that decaying bay, where the distant islands were the colour of cigarette smoke, hand in hand we trudged. Our shoes crunched against the granite shards, and you said: when I am gone from your life, Mr Hendrix, there will be great storms, days of rain and longing. Men will fight. A dark thread will slide from your sandwich. A bat will tamper with your perception. You will come to believe it really existed and that I fed it beetles and worms. Don't be ridiculous, I said. And we walked on, mute, in the direction of our story's very visible end.

LEYTONSTONED

Where shall we go? Mohammed asks. The car is a silver Fiat Quibble, with Cadillac fins, retro boosters and punk upholstery. Los Angeles, says Douglas. I've always wanted to go there. Don't be ridiculous, snorts Mohammed, whispers Mohammed, Mohammed nods. Even if it floated, this car would never get across the Atlantic. We'd run out of legendary gasoline. Also consider the breakers, the sperm whales, the World War Two hedgehog mines. We'd break up. We'd sink and go down. Go down, down, down, all the way to Davy Jones's slurred place. Be realistic, Doug. I say Scotland. I've always wanted to go to Scotland. The tartan transvestites. The Loch Ness monster. Castles on little islands. My aunty has a Views of Scotland calendar. It's lovely. Sure, Scotland, why not? If you're sure the fins aren't retracted wings. I was certain I saw a bone structure there the other day. Perhaps feathers. I'm almost positive I saw some movement there when I looked in the rear view on Tuesday. Remember Tuesday? So how do we get there? You know how to get to the Green Man? I'll direct you from there. Cigarette, my man? The turbine vibrated. Condensation dripped from the windshield. Thanks, squire. Mohammed ducked to avoid a fragment of Sonnet 77 (the first line, he realized, as it shot past with a crackling noise). Mohammed wore a leather shirt with tassle fringes. An hour later they are past Stansted and heading north for the A1(M). There was lassitude in plenty. Look at that! What? Mohammed is hunched over the steering wheel. He seems to be staring at the dashboard. In the sky. That plane. A jumbo. It looks like it's going to crash. It's so close. Nah, it's just landing. They come in low. Like at Heathrow. If you say so. Cigarette, squire? I don't mind if I do. They reach the A1 (M). Its four lanes have almost no traffic. Then it narrows and turns into the A1. Roundabouts appear like blood clots in an artery. Fancy a slug of whisky? Douglas unscrews the cap, takes a few glugs, and offers it to Mohammed. Are you corrupting me, squire? No, I'm offering you whisky. But it won't be any hassle if I have to fight this thing myself. Hand it over. Mohammed takes more than Doug, Doug can't help noticing. Later they stop at a service station for a piss. Here, for two pesetas, they gorge themselves on beer and shrimps and a paella of rice, sweet peppers, saffron, snails, crawfish and little eels. As they eat they watch the local fishermen sitting in their black felucca-rigged boats watching a DVD of *Jaws*. Yorkshire is dreary, with views of distant slagheaps and a bunch of cooling towers on their left. A nuthatch whistles from a derelict paragraph. The sun, becoming warmer and warmer, drinks off the dew, and what were once tall candlesticks, silvery with white bloom, are now tall jade candlesticks of leaves beneath the blue cathedral of a sky leaking from the pen of William Faulkner. It's not long before they are in the border country. Here the air is fresh and translucent.

Leytonstoned

The young grass glows with a happy emerald brilliance. The ringing voice of the chiff-chaff resounds overhead. Shortly afterwards they go under a bridge where someone has spraypainted 'Blair is a cunt'. Now the trees fuse into large blackening masses. An oriole gives a sad cry. Soon they reach the Great Glen. Look at that! The monster! Mohammed says: I can't see it. Where? Over there, by the castle! Three enormous humps. A head like a dragon! Fucking fantastic! Wow, yeah. Cool. A little over a third of a matador's sword, properly placed, will kill a dragon that is not too big. Half a sword will reach the aorta of even the biggest dragon. St George taught me that. Cool. Hey, look! There's the Queen Mother! She's dead, idiot. There's the ghost of the Queen Mother! Sort of luminous! She's ascending to heaven! And they're playing that Led Zeppelin song! How very retro. Can't we have something more modern? Where's the Eels tape? Jack borrowed it. Anyway it wouldn't work in this car, remember? Damn Jack. Where is he these days, anyway? In Sheffield, I expect. That's where his girlfriend lives. Ooh, look! That sign. 'Sheffield 4 miles.' Let's go there now. OK, guv. But Sheffield is empty. No sign of Jack anywhere. There was complete silence in Jack's girlfriend's room. Somewhere in the same building a gramophone began to play. It played and played. Something sweet and onomatopoeic by Mendelssohn, full of waves breaking in echoing caverns. I think one of those bombs must have been dropped. The sort that kills people but doesn't damage property. The ideal American bomb. As a matter of fact I think one's been dropped in Leytonstone. I can't see anyone in the street, can you? And no cars being driven. That's weird. No it's not. Colworth Street is always like this. The road humps put people off. None of these cars go anywhere. You look tomorrow. Mine will still be here. And so will Mr Smith's outside his house. And that couple next door with the camper van. That never moves. Yeah well obviously yours will still be here tomorrow, Mohammed. It's because you've taken the fucking battery out. What I want to know is if it's ever coming back. That battery. So's we can really go somewhere. Shouldn't think so. Who needs a battery? I like sitting here. As that Shakespeare song says, all you gotta do is dream. Plato. You what? Greek bloke. He said everything was a dream. He was right. Anyway, I better go. My uncle wants me to help out in his fucking shop at four. Better do it, for the sake of family values. Also with luck I can nick some ciggies. Coming? Nah, think I'll stay here and finish the spliff. What will you say if he catches you appropriating his cigarettes? Forgive me, dearest uncle! It was an error. I vow never to do this again! A wilfulness in my nature has drawn this calamity down upon me! But it was not intentional. Can you pardon me? O wound not my agonizing soul! Incidentally, Doug, you bloody well remember to lock the door when you go. I don't want people pissing in my car. Will do. Douglas waves goodbye and settles back into the passenger seat. He closes his eyes. The heat of Los Angeles beats against the windshield. The bass frequency of his heart is murky and rich. Observing the steady fall of the barometer he realises there is some dirty weather knocking about. Yes, it was the sweetest thing, that hyperventilating day. You helped the chokes to go away. Iron in my soul, a bloodied hole. Blue collar rhythms and muscular spasms. Aeroplane glue, what's it to you? Gastric juices and toxic sluices, elephant milk and faraway ruses. Overcome by

Leytonstoned

mist and a voice that hissed. Let me tell you, let me toil you. Let me trick you, let me spoil you. Tales of girls and all that fails. That arch in Whitby, a girl named Anne. Of empty rooms, capsules at night. A total absence of delight. Bleached bones, beached whales and all that fails. Fish paste and dirty fingernails. Drunken laughter and mornings after. Emaciation and dehydration. Hepatitis, then bronchitis. Descriptions of repeat prescriptions. Doctor's appointments and pills and ointments. Bouncing cheques and sunken cheeks. Fried afternoons, injected moons. The dentistry and the sophistry. Dynamite banana and *Futurama*. Political tosh, economy wash. Bloody feuds and posturing dudes. Shivers and slivers and rivers and liver. Sallow skin and a cheesy grin. Dandruff showers and springtime flowers. Hairsprays and clichés and two-thrubber frith. Cough syrup brands and punk rock bands. Jubbs and dubs. Quaaludes and preludes. A kneeling nude, a moment lewd. Mona Lisa, just a teaser. Ultrasound scans and wedding banns. R. Budd Dwyer and the dyer's hand. Methadone and Al Capone. Sound box and detox and all of the gold locks. Exhaustion, contortion, and narrative impairment. Ink penitentiary, blue velvet stationery. Coke-snorting daughters and tabloid reporters. Prefab and rehab and rosewater blubber. Musicians' physicians. Empty TV and vacant sky. Irreversible heart disease, the lees. Backwards, down the birth canal. In The Cusp of Modernity we drank ourselves sick, took some stick. Then headed for the Red Dragon, off the wagon. That's where you'd find me then, you bet. Listening to the Cliff Trotsky Quartet. But not now. Here's why, here's how. Rape allegation, the self-perpetuating Central Committee's obfuscation. This is where it ends, comrades and friends. Stalinism and schism. Denial, delusion, a pitiful conclusion.

QUIN AGAIN

THAT WRITER YOU LIKE, says Vee. It says here she's dead. Vee passes over the paper. Novelist found drowned. Novelist found drowned, a few paltry facts. Quin is dead. A great sense of shock runs through me. It is like being scalded in your heart. I look again at the crumbs of data. Quin's body has been recovered. Her body has been identified. And it all begins. On a bright August morning it begins. A long hot day lies ahead of me. Soon Vee goes off to work, leaving me alone in the apartment. I make a second mug of coffee and take Quin's four books from the bookcase. I spend the morning reading extracts and making notes. In the afternoon I walk into town and do some shopping. Vee returns at six for the meal I've cooked. Afterwards she watches TV while I read in another room. We go to bed, to sleep. Night envelops the Quin-shattered city. Everything is fissured now, cracked by her going. She was too young. I drift off, and the shore grows distant. Quin's face stares into mine. I whisper to her and she seems to smile. The starry floor, the watery shore, is given thee till the break of day. Farewell.

As for the rest. Much is still obscure. Quin's reputation dipped to the ocean's bed, where it lingered for several decades before rising cloudily, gently, upward. One day there will be a biography.

Vee and I split up, as you know. Years later she discovered she was a lesbian and now lives very happily with her partner on a hillside in Nice, not far from the Matisse museum. As for Tollinger. He never married, never had children. He moved to London, where he heard bombs explode and witnessed the bloody aftermath of a stabbing. His hair dropped away and his waistline expanded. His face began to resemble the texture of W. H. Auden's. The sound of sirens and furiously shrieking lovers broke open Tollinger's nights and began to wear him down. He left the city and retreated to the coast. He can often be seen on the beach at Sole Bay, by the headland of twisted pines, taking photographs of things that are broken or worn smooth by salt water and gales.

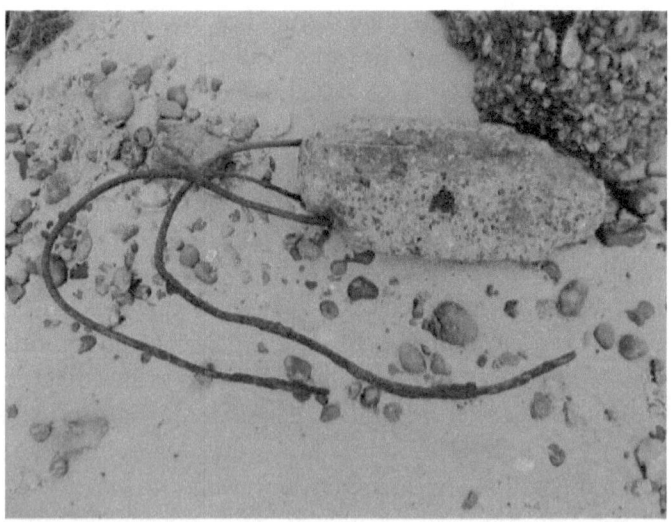

Quin Again

1: Blue

WHERE ARE YOU now? Walking along a street? I followed you with my eyes when you walked away through the crowd and I wanted to run after you and then people pushed me on... All I could think of then was the moment when I will see you emerging from a door or a crowd.

Quin wrote those words. And she never did get to see me emerging from a door or a crowd, because she went away from me and never came back. When, later, I emerged from doors or crowds, it was to greet other women. Never Quin.

I will now answer Quin's first question, which has hung over me all through the long years. Where am I? I am in a seaside town, here on the crumbling coastline of East Anglia. And I feel blue. And I like it here, because everything is also blue. Blue is where it ends. Blue because blue is taking everything away. Take a look for yourself. The blue sea is eating the white cliffs. See? The cliffs are to the east, where a cold wind blows in from that land beyond the ocean. Cold, very cold. The blue sea splits the towering chalk. The town itself is built on other cliffs, which are sealed over with concrete. A nineteenth century esplanade runs below this concrete escarpment. The esplanade drops down to the beach. See? There, on the grey sand, the blue sea breaks.

Call me Tollinger. It's not my real name but it will do. I came to this place because of Quin. And I came because it might as well end here as anywhere. Because, after many, many years, Quin is finally coming back to me.

I find the decay and the desolation here congenial. I enjoy watching rust weep. This entire town is weeping.

Grief drips from drain pipes and gutters. Entropy is everywhere. I keep close to the kerb because on windy nights tiles sometimes tumble from the rooftops of the Victorian terraces. Black flakes explode beside me, scattering razorblades and needles. This is a town with many fences and concrete posts. The posts are studded with bolts. The bolts weep orange tears. I like it here. I like to hear the gulls scream on the ledges by the broken windows of the derelict buildings. And this is where it will end, when Quin finally arrives. I won't make old bones, this I know.

And blue because blue is where I am done with words. For the moment they are unavoidable and I must void them. For the moment they cling to me like drops of moisture in a hot, poorly ventilated room. But I shall shed them in the end, as all must. A last whisper, a little groan, then silence. Nothing more to say, nothing more to look at. Eyes dead as those of a cemetery angel.

In the meantime I wait for Quin and death. I kill it, quietly, time. I spend day after day alone in my apartment. It's one of two on the top floor of an old house marooned on a corner of the road which runs along the eastern edge of the town. There are other tenants of the house but I almost never see them. How do I pass my days? As in everything I do: quietly, obscurely. *Je suis un marginal.* I read books. I watch old Robert Mitchum movies. I have an ambition to view every film Mitchum ever made. I know this will not be achieved. I listen to music through my Sennheiser noise-cancelling headphones. Music has always been important to me. Bach's Cantata #50 performed by Mimi Coertse, Margaret Sjöstedt, Hilde Rössl-Majdan, Anton Dermota, Frederick Guthrie and the Choir and Orchestra of the

Quin Again

Vienna State Opera, say. Neil Young's *Time Fades Away*, say. *Anticipation. Goat's Head Soup. She Used To Wanna Be a Ballerina. Die Zauberflöte. New Skin for the Old Ceremony. Desire, Hard Rain. Blue.* I have measured out my life with them. And how should I begin to take the measurements?

By blue, I suppose. Blue because blue is taking everything away. Cocusa blue, for all that is lost to me. Blue for the colour of my memories. Blue the perfect sky, a backdrop to all my imperfections. Blue for that notorious depleted satellite. Cocusa blue, for everything.

When he does anything at all, Tollinger goes out for a walk or to the shops. There are three basic walking routes. Tollinger can head east, along the cliff top walk, to the lighthouse. There are steps there which lead down to the beach.

Or Tollinger can descend to the shingle and sand and go westward, as far as the fossil forest and the derelict fairground. Or Tollinger can simply wander the town, strolling along broad avenues of decaying villas, where the gardens are filled with palm trees and streaky bamboo. This town has a flint-walled church, which inside is cold and bare as death. Brasses display data about dead imperial warriors.

This church was once two miles from the sea. Now it is close to the edge. As is the Hotel de Paris, a century-old hotel. The hotel overlooks the pier, which puts on shows. I have no interest in these shows. But even if I did desire to see the comedian or the variety show or the elderly rockers, I would not go. Not to a show. At a show you are vulnerable. You have no control over what is happening behind you. I do not want my life to end at a show. It must either be in a silent room or on a deserted beach. Just the two of us. Quin, with her weapon. Her victim calm and co-operative. The fuss kept to a minimum.

Blue because blue is taking everything away. Including my cognitive abilities. My mind isn't what it was. I am starting to forget things. I am starting to confuse things. I am starting to lose the names of objects and people. I am beginning to wonder if Quin is really who I think she is. But I have her books. I will always have her books. My priceless editions. I keep them hidden. They must never be touched by the contagion of the wind and the rain or the borrowers... I must not let blue lap at their dustjackets.

Let me say this about Quin. One day she was not there and the next day she was there. And then, later, one day she was there, and the next day she was not there. This is what happens between lovers. And now? Now your Tollinger is exhausted. Now poor old Tollinger's muscles ache. My skin, like my mind, is beginning to ripple and wrinkle. Physical decrepitude is on its way. It is hard to get excited like in the old days. All the mysteries are gone

Quin Again

from me. And I have grown tired of running. This is my last refuge.

Quin has always been everywhere for yours truly. Ever since that summer when she disappeared forever. Tollinger thought he glimpsed Quin in Biarritz. Tollinger walked past the Musée de la Mer and he was almost certain he saw her in the nearby tunnel. Later Tollinger walked across the curving beach while the surf exploded beside him. Tollinger was convinced it was her sat on an iron bench on a distant hotel balcony. As soon as Quin saw him watching she went indoors. The next day Tollinger was positive he saw her walking near *le rocher de la Vierge*. On each of these occasions she slipped away from him, just as she had done all those years earlier. Tollinger thought he saw her on the little ferry in Concarneau. She was crossing to the town and Tollinger called out 'Quin! It's me!' But though I am certain she heard me she kept her back turned.

How long have I been here, hiding out in this rotting seaside town? A good question. Thirty-five years, can you believe? Hard to credit. Although it seems like only yesterday I strolled out of the Hotel de Paris, suitcase in hand. My jacket was blue, my heart was ablaze, I was so happy. What a fine, lusty young swaggerer I was back then! I walked to the blue car and put the case inside. Quin drove me north. We were headed for Cape Wrath. It was a long drive. That was thirty-five years ago. And yet that summer seems like only last month.

I howled her name. I still do. I talked in my sleep. I still do. I cried out for her. That, too. I ground my teeth. But Quin kept her back turned, her eyes averted. She shut me out. The ferry's wake reached the shore and shook its accumulations of weed. It stirred up a little

Concarneau mud. Quin kept her back turned and the hours turned into decades. Dust poured down from the desert. The floor cracked. I went back to look at number 44 in Finchley and everything was grey and cold. I looked at the window, which was still the same shape. The same lace curtains. But the patch of grass between our window and the street had been concreted over, for parking a small car. The fabric of the past was a thin, tattered thing. The props were looking worn. A cold wind was gusting in from the west. I walked quickly back to the underground, consumed by heartbreak. Shut it, Tollinger. Shut it and keep walking. Shut it and keep talking. Squirt some words. Keep the darkness at bay.

Some youths were just now in the street at the back, making a youth racket. One of them had a tin drum, which he was beating with monotonous regularity. Two others were breaking bottles. They had girl attachments. I shouted at them, asked what they were up to. 'We're making background noise,' a girl said. She had lurid red hair and lips. Her face was coated in a white paste. She wore a black duffel coat. She was into vampires, I could tell.

I used to dream of going to the far north. I still dream of Cape Wrath. On that long drive north there is a cave. It would be a good place to live out what little left remains. I discovered it years ago with Quin. She parked the blue car in a lay-by and we set, off hand in hand through a pine forest. We were so happy we should have been in a commercial. Life was sweet, we couldn't keep our hands off each other. It was bliss to be alive. We trod softly across the pine needles. Something moved in the shadows up ahead. A big sensitive deer. It sensed our presence and cantered off. A little later we came across the rest of the herd. They nosed us and fled. We were trespassing on an aristocratic estate. I remember a burbling stream and rocks coated in emerald moss. We emerged from the forest and crossed a meadow. Then it was a hard slog up an ancient volcanic slope. We came to the tip of the cliff and looked down. There was a grassy undercliff and beyond it the lake. A massive blue trench cutting north-by-north-west to its opposite. I helped her down the slope. And that was when we discovered it. The cave. About the width and height of a bus, but fringed by growth and curtained by creepers and not at all obvious until you were right by it. A dark vulva in the crag's crotch.

A year later I was in Africa. Quin had gone from my life. The tropical night had rushed in. The stars were astonishing. So bright, so close, so animated. Such multiplicities. The Milky Way revived the desire to go on. I lay there all night. Shapes like lions prowled the scorched perimeter, then drifted away. The embers all around me ticked like an old clock. The darkness was filled with slitherings and whispers and the shuffle of unidentifiable creatures. I woke from uneasy dreams to a blue sky, blazingly bright, as searing as Quin's love for me and my love for her. I walked north. I rested in the shadow of an inselberg. I paid a tribesman to drive me over the border. A week later I was in Chamonix. After Africa I was in the mood for ice and snow and glaciers and cold, cracked things.

I must now make a report. It is very urgent. Listen to me! More blue spore has fallen! I have seen it with my own eyes. I saw it first on the second Tuesday after I arrived here. I was on the clifftop walk. It was late afternoon. The sun shot three rays from out of a cigar-shaped silver cloud. The grass in the fields rippled like waves. In the cold light I saw it, a vast slow drift of blue shadow. It fell over the town and was gone. The buildings were touched by a bruised pallor, then quickly returned to normal. When I went back into town some people were still wiping it from their clothing. The spore left a dull smear. And now everyone is turning into automatons. There are few of us left who are not diseased. The movies were there ahead of us. The movies knew how the end would be. The police are rotten. They cannot be trusted. The police are working for the spore. In order not to attract their attention it is important to walk in a slow, measured manner. Express no emotion. Do not take any interest in any disturbance you may witness on the street. Take no photographs. Keep walking, keep calm. Ignore the eviction. There must be no laughter or screaming. Everything must be kept within the parameters of the normal. Display your disease. Display your trim hair, neat suit and well-manicured nails. There must be no gnawing, no scowling. Good grooming is essential in establishing your diseased citizenship. Show that you are subservient to the great order. You must pretend to fall asleep but underneath you must remain alert to what is happening all around you. This is not easy when there is television and alcohol and sex. If you fail in this they will not be fooled. Under Section Two, you can be detained for up to twenty-eight days. Significantly longer under Section Three. You may call upon a Second Opinion Appointed Doctor – a SOAD – who is appointed by the Mental Health Act Commission. If the second doctor agrees with the first doctor then electro-convulsive therapy may be compulsory. You are free to leave once your doctor is pleased with you. You are free once they have broken down your resistance and you can be trusted to take the pills.

I have concluded that it is better to die quickly than to drift into a half-life. Quin's arrival will be a mercy. A great weight will have been lifted. The morphine she brings will be sweet. The bodkin she smilingly slides into my heart will barely be felt. I shall crumple gracefully to the floor. In my dying moments I shall stare at Q's scarlet pumps. The Fugue in B Minor will continue as the camera tracks away, down the stairs, into the street, where cars move and people walk to and fro, and life goes on, as it does, forgetting you. And blue is the colour of *Glenn Gould: The Italian Album*. The last track in my imaginary movie is always Fugue in B Minor on a theme by Tomaso Albinoni. Soft as the blue sea on the day that Quin arrives. Low as the breaking of those blue waves. As calm as Quin as she fills the hypodermic. She holds it up and examines the fluid inside. She does this because she, too, has seen all the necessary movies. There are certain conventions of behaviour which must not be breached. We all live for the imagery. She stabs it into my blue vein. Her green eyes regard me tenderly as I begin to move away from the harbour wall. The current grips me in its muscle. I relax inside its flexure. I am happy happy blue. I stand with my back to the cliff. Quin aims at my heart and shoots. I jerk backwards, arms spread wide like a man on a cross. I fly forwards and fall. The camera looks down at the motionless shape on the shingle below. C/U of the dripping scalp, hairs stirred by the breeze. As the camera tracks away to the sea, the Fugue begins. A blue shadow falls across the waves. THE END. And then, in italic copperplate: *Inspired By Real*

Events.

Quin published four books. I shall call them *One*, *Two*, *Three* and *Four*.

With each novel, she pushed at the boundaries. *One* is set in a seaside town. The ambiance is one of squalor, impoverishment and degradation. *Two* is about a couple and a missing third person. *Three* is fractured and hot.

Quin Again

Four scorches across the disunited states.

Why am I in this particular decayed seaside resort? Is it because of Vee? It's certainly strange to think that I once lived in this town with Vee. Once Vee meant everything to me, but that was before I knew Quin. Now decades have rolled and Vee is also long gone. Her blue beads broke and she went off to other bedrooms, other beds. Quin, too, of course, yet it's Quin who haunts and torments me, not Vee. I almost never think of Vee. Quin is the woman who broke my heart. Quin is the woman I can't free my mind from. Quin's words hang around me like chains. I am so full of your presence that my eyes keep brimming over and I hear your voice in my ears and feel your hands on my body and all the words I say express only a minute fraction of what I feel, she wrote. That was before she decided we couldn't go on being lovers. That was just before she swam away and drowned herself in a cold ocean of time.

Forgive me. I am becoming maudlin. I am straying off topic. (Straying! Ah, did I ever take Quin to The Stray when I persuaded her to spend a night in Harrogate? I don't remember. Harrogate is a distant blur.)

Let's return to the facts. Once I lived here in this town. Veronika Freie was my lover. My beloved Vee. Quin does not know that. Gotz knew that, I am certain. I am sure I told her. But Quin never knew. Quin will track me down and find me, but not because of the Vee connection. Vee died a long time ago, taking things with her that only she and I knew. So blue for the sky that burns above but which will shortly darken and fill with pricks of light. Pricks of light which will shine down on this little room where I lie dying, dying. Blue for this spore-sodden town, this wailing coastline, this block of words. Words where it ends, the action. Blue the shimmering sea scrap which I see from this window. Blue for Quin's arrival. Quin is on her way. Her blue arrival will punctuate it, this sentence of life.

Vee looks up from breakfast. She holds out the newspaper. 'Look,' she says. 'That woman writer you are always going on about it. She's dead. It says here she was found drowned.' It was the end of August of that year. A summer which lies across my life like a slab. August is where it always ends. This have I learned. This knowledge is cut deep into my old skin. And a long bitter winter has to be endured before there is any possibility of a new bitter beginning. That's a sentence I ought to delete but probably won't.

I remember that summer, very vividly. It was just before I followed Vee to the seaside. It was the summer Quin went away. The house where I lived with Vee was on a corner, at a junction. We rented the top half. You opened the door and were at once faced by two doors – a cheap metaphor for every human destiny. The door to the downstairs flat was on the right. The door to the upstairs flat was on the left. Left, and up those stairs. The lay-out is faded and I took no photographs. There was a small box room with a single bed, located above the stairs. Adjacent to that was what must have been the living room, or perhaps another bedroom. In memory it is a void. I seem to remember a small kitchen. I remember it lacked a refrigerator and the meat I bought had to be eaten that day, otherwise it began to smell. It was a hot summer, a claustrophobic summer. I distinctly remember a small bathroom. Was there a bath? I feel sure there must have been but I am not certain. I remember a toilet. I remember a frosted glass window.

Quin Again

But if you go back and look there is no window where that window should be. After all these years the house is still there and it looks exactly the same – except there is no bathroom window. Was it bricked up? Did I imagine it? Impossible now to tell. The bedroom is altogether more memorable. I remember a double bed, a dressing table with a mirror, a television. But what did we say to each other all that summer? The conversations have drained away. I remember none of them. What did we do? I suppose we went out and saw movies, but I recall none. What I remember most is being in bed on Saturday afternoons, watching TV. Or to be more precise, I remember going to bed with Vee on Saturday afternoons and after sex we would lie there and watch *Star Trek*.

It was a hot summer, a claustrophobic summer. Vee went out to work each day, while I read and wrote and did the shopping and the cooking. Some days I met her at lunchtime at the pub at the end of Unthank Road. I am almost certain it was called The Three Tuns but though it still exists the name has changed. But perhaps it was not Vee I met there. Perhaps it was someone else. Perhaps that is where I first met Quin. Yes, I remember now. I had been there since the place opened at eleven. I was staring at the rising galaxy in my pint glass when a figure appeared, stark in the doorway. An aura of light framed her dark silhouette. For a moment I thought she was nude. Quin was wearing yellow boots, yellow trousers, a flesh-coloured blouse. Her voice trembled. 'I'm so cold,' she said. 'So very, very cold.' It seemed an odd thing to say. It was a hot morning in August. The sky was blue and cloudless. A heat haze made the cathedral shimmer. But then I saw that she was drenched. The texture of her pants clung to her thighs. Her blouse followed the contours of her small, firm breasts. She did not appear to be wearing a bra. Her nipples were very distinct. Quin wore a pair of very large sunglasses. I bought her a gin and tonic, and then three more. Soon she was warmed up. Back at the apartment she slipped out of her sodden clothes and took a hot bath. I hung her wet clothes on Vee's horse. Quin's knickers entranced me with their pattern of daisies and their enticing tang of salt marsh. Later she opened the bathroom door and stepped out inside a surge of steam. She'd wrapped a blue towel around herself. She steadied herself against a bookcase. She reached behind herself and slackened the knot. The towel dropped to the floor. Quin stood before me with flushed cheeks. Her pubic hair was moderate in substance. 'Let's fuck,' she said. This is an invitation I never refuse. I peeled away my shirt and jeans. She writhed beneath me. When her pleasure was spent I speeded up the engine of my lust. Three hours later Vee returned and found me in bed, naked and tired and irritable. She suspected nothing. She attributed my condition to a weakness for alcohol and a fondness for masturbation. I dressed and took Vee out to a Greek restaurant. I told her jokes and made her laugh.

The next day I met up with Quin and showed her round the city. My memory of that day is a little hazy. Only a single photograph survives. Now I don't even recall what it is she's holding in her hands. It resembles a calendar. I would have liked her to return to the apartment for another frolic, but she said this would not be possible. 'Fare thee well for I must leave thee,' she said. Then it was time for her to go. I walked with her to the gate. She went through it and became lost among the other passengers. I turned away, my vision blinded by

Quin Again

tears. I never saw her again. She had decided to drown herself in the years.

I remember how once we went to a pub on Earlham Road but I no longer remember which one. I told her my favourite film was *Carnival of Souls*. Quin smiled serenely. She, too, agreed that this was the best movie ever made.

There are six apartments, here in this rotting mansion which will be my last address. On the ground floor are Mr and Mrs Bray, a broken white couple, very old and chalky. They are retired. I quite often see Mrs Bray cleaning the hallway. She worships Dettol, she told me so herself. It is so kind of her to clean the hallway because no one else would bother. I certainly wouldn't. I have never objected to dust or dirt. Also on the ground floor is a black man I hardly ever see. He is tall and thin and only seems to go out at night. He is probably a criminal or a vampire. On the first floor, close to the stairs, is a property developer named Tim. I know he is a property developer because I can hear what he is saying on the telephone. Sometimes we pass on the stairs and nod indifferently at each other. He wears a frock coat. He has an old fashioned landline by his front door and through the frosted glass I can see him, swaying, gesticulating as he shouts about a really great little property. He must be dodgy because no successful business person would operate out of decrepit and shady premises like these. On this floor there is also a woman I have never seen. She seems to live alone. Sometimes I hear her hoovering the carpet. I know it is a woman because often I hear her crying. She is in the aftermath of something but I don't know what. A bereavement? I imagine a dead child. A freckled lad, seven, a speeding drunk. I imagine a hard-working decent husband with cancer. I envisage the end of a relationship. Her brute of

Quin Again

a husband has dumped her for his secretary, who is young and blonde and who will shortly give birth to his child. Or her husband has run off with her big-breasted best friend, who is feisty and freckly and filthy and fun. Or perhaps she is simply lonely and single and unfulfilled, as so many are.

On the top floor is me. And two other tenants. A couple whom I hardly ever see. They cohabit behind the door opposite. She is a ripe redhead, he is sleek and square-jawed and oily. They leave early in the morning and return late at night. They are rowdy at weekends when they play loud music. Their relationship seems to thrive on quarrelling. I hear them screaming foul abuse at each other. And then silence. It's a routine. The yelping of obscenities, then thumps and crashes and rustlings. Then silence. The silence is followed by her orgasm. She is a howler. Even the Brays probably hear her come. But the howling has a theatrical quality. It is a little too vigorous and sustained to be entirely convincing. Sometimes I catch scraps of improbable dialogue. They are acting to a Hollywood script. Once all this would have driven me to a frenzy. But not now. Desire's theatricals are quite played out for me. Let me be alone on my little stage. Let me start a scene or two, no more than that. Leave me in the shadow of the wings, intoning cryptic brief soliloquies. Entropy, departure, sadness. Here in Cocusa we have a word for my condition: *odcházeni*.

The sea here is a shade of blue that is good enough to drown in. Cocusa blue. My psychiatrist says she is very interested by what I am writing down. So is Dr Martin. She revealed that Dr Martin had filched one of my old manuscripts. After reading *Reminiscences of a Dancing*

Man he concluded that I was not yet fit for parole.

I hissed that he was a fascist, and she smiled ambiguously. 'As for these feverish fantasies of yours about a psychiatrist...' 'They are not fantasies. I'm not writing about you but someone else. It was all a very long time ago. And yet, curiously, it as fresh as yesterday.' 'You are beginning to repeat yourself,' she said in words as crisp as her white cotton blouse. The outline of her black bra was very distinct. When she leaned forward to write in her pad I caught a glimpse of cleavage and a wisp of exquisite perfume. My penis sprang up and swayed for a few seconds, before quickly returning to the posture of an exhausted snake. 'You do realise that "Cocusa" does not exist, don't you?' 'It does exist! I once spent a night there with Quin!' I replied. 'Ah, yes,' she said sadly. 'Quin. Tell me about this woman Quin.'

That winter I stayed on, alone. Vee was living further along the coast and no longer shared my nights. I listened to that year's new Rolling Stones album. I went for long walks in the grey. I read the new translation by Martin Nicolaus – the first complete translation into English – of the *Grundrisse*.

The other day I had an idea for a short story. It would be a story structured around three old Stones albums. This narrative would need to be concealed at all times from Dr Martin. The first album in the story, *Goat's Head Soup*, would commemorate that long winter when things started to go wrong with Veronika Freie. Badly wrong. Very badly wrong. The second, *Black and Blue*, would celebrate that unforgettable summer with Quin. The last one, *Some Girls*, would be about going clear. My conception is titled 'Granite Heart: A story in three albums.' I shall never write it. I am finished with short stories. They bore me. All true stories are long stories. Having said that, let me add that this does not signify that a narrative has to suffer from Proteus syndrome. The best fiction is the length of a novella. I establish this scientifically and irrefutably with reference to *La Jalousie, Black Sunlight, Intolerable Tongues, Lunar Caustic* and *Transparent Things*. Not forgetting – *never* forgetting – my own sweet darling's *Three*.

I have tried to take an interest in the science of my condition. But I learn nothing I do not already know. And what good is understanding? Knowledge doesn't cure the pain.

MEMORY IS THE RESULT of a storing-up of impressions in our minds by which we are able to recognize these impressions when they present themselves again. Many elderly people have an excellent memory for things which happened long ago, but things which have only recently occurred are forgotten because their brains are unable to receive any more mental impressions.

Memory fails in many disorders of the mind. Loss of memory is a striking feature of general paralysis of the insane.

See also: INSANITY, MELANCHOLIA and MENTAL HYGIENE.

I sink into stories to pass the dead hours. I lose myself in stories to forget my own story. Fiction is the morphine of the dying. Fiction will soothe you by making sense of everything. The book had a blue cover. That was the only reason I was attracted to it. I bought it from the remainder shop on Terminal Road. The white-cheeked teenage girl at the counter was reading a vampire book. Its cover was red, purple and black, which occluded further interest on my part.

On the first page of my blue book I read of Porlock, whose name was not his own. There was a murder. The Inspector had deep-set, lustrous eyes. The Manor House in which the corpse was discovered dated back to the time of the first crusade. It was still much as the builder had left it in the seventeenth century. The only approach to the house was over a drawbridge, raised every evening and lowered every morning. There was blood on the sill. There was a quaint, gnarled dried-up person, who was the butler. There was a tall, formal, melancholy man who was the village sergeant. The deadlock was broken by a woman's voice. It was a singular and terrible narrative. It unravelled so long and dark a train of events. At the end there was a savage twist and then the uplift of an explanation.

Quin Again

2: Reminiscences of a Dancing Man

A VILLAGE HALL, made of corrugated iron. Bleating sheep wandering around, drifting across the narrow, winding road. Masses of ferns and bracken, the hillsides rising up sharply. The summits tipped with gold. The sun sinking lower. Right went back to the road to Fort William, left went on beside the loch. Left was a dead end; it led nowhere. Left. A grey church rising up behind a massive hedge; close by it, a deserted jetty; beyond, a distant view of low, wooded islands. The loch looked short and round and shallow. An illusion; most of it lay beyond the chain of islands a mile off. A long, dark trench reaching back into the barren interior. A loch to parallel Nevis, about the same size.

The road followed the loch side, then continued straight on while the land bulged out to the south, and the loch faded from view. A switchback road: up and down and up and down. The occasional house, far back from the road. The road passed over the last rolling hill and the main body of the loch became visible, stretching away to the east. Its end out of sight, lost behind a headland. The tarmac road lasted for another mile, then ended. There was a turning space, but we kept going along a bumpy track encrusted with small rocks. Quin said nothing.

Something crashed against the underside of the car. Probably the exhaust, taking a battering. The track lasted a few hundred yards, then opened into a flat, grassy area about the size of a football pitch. On the far side a path continued on along the lochside, but it was far too narrow for a car. The mountain sides had lost their bronze colour now, and looked grey and desolate. The sky was darkening rapidly. The stars were starting to come out, hundreds of them, thousands, until the sky was a vast bowl of glittering, sparkling dots, far brighter and more intense than anything I'd ever known in the city. Wavelets slapped a thin strip of shingle. The loch seemed vast and brooding and full of secrets. Style and language were such a comfort to me then.

It was going to be another lovely sunny day in Cocusa. From somewhere in the fells high above came the bleating of sheep. The sky was velvet blue, the loch mirroring it. The loch flat calm. A solitary white swan

Quin Again

came gliding round the nearest headland, its head held erect. A black wake spread slowly behind it. The path on the far side turned inland, following the course of a stream. It crossed a stone bridge and twisted back towards the loch. Waist-high ferns hemmed us in on both sides. Quin said: 'We shall drown in green.' I nodded. Turn away no more, my love. The starry floor, the watery shore, is given thee till the break of day.

A blue butterfly, skipping between neurotic thistles. The path here broadens and curves eastward, rising until it's about twenty yards above the surface of the loch. It follows the shoreline. On the map the loch looked like a straight, narrow, elongated rectangle. In reality the shore was a series of crescent-shaped bays, divided by small promontories. Each bay and promontory led on to a view of the next one, while the end of the loch seemed to remain always just out of sight. We walked on and came to a ruined croft. It had almost vanished under a surge of vegetation. Once this place had sustained a scattered population. Now it was as desolate and deserted as the moon. Quin stood in a ruined room, staring through a ruined glass-less window. Grass rose up around her ankles. I shall come back here one day, I thought. Alone. When this is all over.

The further we went, the more the fells came closer. A steep wall of rock rising up to the left of the grassy path. As the sun came out from beyond the mountains it turned the surface of the loch to a glittering, blinding sheet of silver. I slipped on my Ray-Bans and kept going, meeting no one. Quin had melted from the narrative, but I knew she'd be back. I pressed on with my adventure, my novel ideas. The path rose higher, curving round the edge of a steep-sided bay. There was no beach; the rock slipped sheer into the dark, deep water. The lake had been scooped out in the last ice age; a few yards from the shore it fell sharply to depths of two hundred yards and more. I came round a big, rocky outcrop and suddenly, there ahead of me, the land fell away, the loch widened, and I could see all the way to the end. A blue heat haze had settled over everything, giving the harsh landscape a soft focus.

A faint puttering noise. I turned and looked behind me. At first I could see nothing. Only when I scanned the loch surface with binoculars did I spot the boat. It was a fisherman, chugging along with a little outboard motor. He was about a mile away. As I watched he cut the motor, and the boat started to drift back the way he'd come. Soon he was gone from sight. I went on, passing a promontory of low rock which curled back, forming a natural harbour. Beyond it was a substantial bay, and the path swerved away to the left. Soon the loch dropped out of sight. I walked round a corner and at once a dog started a frenzied barking. Twenty yards ahead of me was a house. It had a garden gate, and roses twining around a yellow wooden front door. A drift of smoke came from a chimney, and somewhere nearby I could hear the sound of hens clucking.

The path went right past the house, alongside a fence. The fence shook as the dog hurled itself against it and continued its yelping. I stepped quickly back out of sight of the house, and hurriedly retraced my steps. Behind me a woman's voice shouted at the dog, which went on barking. I decided to climb up the hillside and cut across behind the house. I went back far enough not to be seen, then started to scramble up the slope. It was steep and tiring but it wasn't particularly difficult or dangerous.

Quin Again

The hillside was tufted with heather and studded with volcanic rock. Two-thirds of the way up I paused and looked back.

A dragonfly flew past, hovered like a miniature surveillance drone, and then shot off again. It was hot, even in the shade. In the distance the heat shimmered up from the loch surface. A tiny speck by one of the islands was the fisherman, still drifting westward. A ghostly finger of smoke rose up from behind the grassy headland which hid the house. In the west, beyond the dark blur of Morar village, I could see a thin blue strip of sea and a line of wispy cirrus. I went on up to the summit, grabbing handfuls of grass and hauling myself up the final steep patch. I didn't look down, though I could hear dislodged stones thumping and cracking as they fell and hit rocks further down the hillside.

When I reached the top I found myself on a vast, flat plateau. It was like being on top of a gigantic table. The other side of the table was miles away. But the flatness was illusory; the land had been eroded by wind and rain for tens of thousands of years. As I started to walk across it I found the plateau was fissured by ditches and rock pools and unexpectedly marshy. There were little gulfs full of darkness and black icy water, and substantial indentations as big as craters which had filled with water to form little lochans. Tufts of wiry weed thrust up out of the water. A pair of scarlet butterflies fluttered past, playing a game of tag. A big drowsy bumblebee drifted by.

I went down into one of the depressions and sat on a rock at the edge of a lochan. There I opened up my map of the Morar region. I had a pretty good idea where I was. The sun has high above me in the sky, squashing my shadow and making me thirsty.

I cut across a corner of the table, and found the valley I was looking for. It was where the lochside path went, for no obvious reason. Instead of continuing on to the end of Morar it turned off and went north, emerging on the shore of Loch Nevis. Maybe once there had been another crofters' settlement there, but if there had it wasn't marked on the map. The valley was bleak and narrow and shady. The path ran along it in a virtually straight line. I kept going, walking fast. After about twenty-five minutes the valley opened out and ahead of me I saw woodland. Just before it, a track descended from the hillside to the left, crossed the footway I was on, and snaked away to my right. Deep tyre prints were embossed in an imaginary section of baked, cracked mud. I decided to ignore the track. I crossed it and kept going. The woodland drew closer.

The path threaded through it, and I caught glimpses of blue up ahead. Soon it emerged on to a narrow shore of pebbles. Ahead of me was a vast stretch of water. I'd come through the mountain pass and I was now once again looking at Loch Nevis. I was further along than I'd been on the road out of Mallaig and I was at sea level now instead of being high up on the hilltop. The path turned left but I decided to go the other way, in the direction of the island. I couldn't see Achnamuirin, but it couldn't be far away. Maybe it was beyond the next headland. I set off along the beach, the pebbles crunching noisily under my feet.

The beach ended at a rock outcrop, and I scrambled up back on to dry land. There was no path here, and it was hard going. Trees grew as far as the water's edge, and I had to push my way through curtain after curtain of branches and leaves. My rucksack kept catching on twigs. The rough, spiky strand of a wild raspberry bush caught my wrist, slashing it and sending half a dozen beads of blood bubbling up. I stopped to wrap my handkerchief around the broken skin. A wasp found me and decided to keep me company. I slapped the air. It seemed to enjoy the game. Eventually it lost interest and headed out across the loch. Round the headland was another bay, another headland, and still no sign of the island. I felt tired. The rucksack, though containing little, was starting to dig into my back and chafe the skin. I dropped down on to the beach and walked to the far end. There I sat down and drank the coffee in my Thermos flask and ate some sandwiches and chocolate. My legs ached. I was out of shape, and I knew it. I was a city animal, not used to long walks in difficult terrain.

Time to move on. I reached the next headland and the far side of it I saw at last, Achnamuirin. It was much closer now; a long, dense slab of greenery rising sheer out of the water, with a slight haze hanging over it. I briefly scanned it through the binoculars, but there were still no signs of life. My angle of vision was different to what it had been earlier. I couldn't see the mock-Tudor house; it must be further round the headland at the western end of the island. Best of all was the sight of a jetty protruding out from the shoreline some four hundred metres further along the beach. Near it was a wooden structure which looked very much like a boathouse. A red and white life belt was attached to a pole nearby.

It took another fifteen minutes of struggling through undergrowth to reach the jetty. It had an air of desolation and emptiness. Waves noisily slapped the stanchions. A cobweb stretched across the life belt; a spider rested in the netting, being gently rocked by the breeze. I saw that the boathouse had a small, dirty window and walked across and peered inside. To my disappointment I saw not a boat but the green, mud-splashed panels of a Land Rover. It was obviously the one I'd seen driven by the blonde woman. It wasn't a boat house at all but a garage. At the back were a pair of padlocked doors. A rough track zigzagged away, rising steeply up behind the trees.

My hopes were dashed. I'd been counting on finding a boat. I sat down and gloomily ate the last of my provisions.

The shadows were starting to lengthen. I decided to head back to my tent and try the coast again tomorrow. There had to be a boat *somewhere*. Maybe I was making a mistake, trying the Nevis shoreline. Maybe I should go back to Morar and see if I could steal a boat from the west-facing coast. On the drive up I'd passed campsite signs and one pointing to Morar Beach. It was worth checking out. I decided against fighting my way back through the barely penetrable undergrowth by the loch shore. Instead I followed the zigzag route up the hillside. It seemed likely that it was the track that crossed the valley footpath I'd walked along earlier. I guessed right. An hour's brisk walking took me back there. Upon meeting it, I turned left, re-tracing my steps. I walked for twenty minutes, then peeled off the footpath and headed up the steep slope. Sweating, I reached the top and set off towards the south west. I reckoned I could save time by cutting across the plateau. That way I'd avoid the serpentine path along the lochside.

The sky became streaky with orange and yellows as

the sun starting sinking towards Skye. The grass and heather started to turn the same colour as the rock which studded them. In the big depressions the lochans were no longer blue but an oily black. For the first time that day I felt a chill in the air. I hurried on back to the western end of the loch. I didn't want to get caught up on the plateau after dark. Too many ditches, too much swamp. I was looking forward to getting back to the car, cooking some warm food, and crawling into the sleeping bag for a good night's sleep. I felt worn out by the day's exertions. I reached the edge of the plateau. I'd done well. Not too far away were the islands which separated the main body of the loch from the lagoon by the village of Morar. The hillside the other side of the loch glowed with the coppery light of the setting sun. Just a few hundred metres away were the fells, dropping almost sheer from the hilltop. I could see the strip of grass beside the loch.

It was no longer empty, as it had been when I'd left this morning. Now there were half a dozen police vehicles parked there. There was a lot of activity by the ruined crofts, and I could see they'd found the Peugeot. There was also the sound of dogs yelping. Their barks rose clearly from below. I stared down and saw a pair of dog handlers with their animals. They were approaching along the lochside path. Twenty or so police officers trudged after them. I backed away from the edge, heart pounding. This was seriously bad news. I had all my stuff down there. Food, tent, *everything*. Worse, the cops now knew I was in the area. I had to get to Achnamuirin at once, have my showdown with Cardew. But how in hell was I going to get there?

Returning to Morar village and finding a boat on the

coast wasn't an option, not now. I retreated back across the plateau. Luckily I still had the compass and the map. I headed for Loch Nevis. I calculated that if the dogs had my scent they wouldn't find a sniff of me until they got to the point in the narrow valley where I'd left the path and scrambled up the slope. That would lead them to where I was now. All the more reason to go north, away from them. The only thing on my side was the hour. The afternoon was fading into dusk. Another hour and it would be night. Unless they had night vision goggles – and they were police, not the army, so I reckoned they wouldn't have – I was safe, for a while at least. I had maybe a two hour lead. They just didn't have time to catch up with me in daylight. Hopefully, when night fell they'd pack in the search. I hurried on.

Darkness caught me first. The yellows in the west diluted and died. A deep rich blue velvet filled the sky. The first stars began to twinkle. The velvet went. I was still trudging across the plateau, walking very slowly and carefully now. The grass was the colour of metal. It became difficult to distinguish grass from rock, rock from pools and ditches and dark, squelchy puddles of swampy ground. I reached the edge of one of the big crater-like depressions. The stars reflected in the dead calm lochan in its base. It was now over an hour since I'd heard the dogs. I hoped their handlers had given up for the day. I hoped the doggies were in their kennels, chewing on a nice juicy bone. The good thing was that I was in a landscape of complete silence and darkness and isolation. No flashlights pierced the night. No one shouted or called. I reckoned I was safe until daylight. I reckoned I'd soon be back at the shore of Loch Nevis. (I had a plan. Return to the shed where the Land Rover was kept. Wait there until the boat came from the island. Hopefully it made regular trips to the mainland. Then hijack the boat. Easy-peasy.) And then, far off in the night behind me, I heard the sound of machinery.

A low, distant droning. As it came closer it turned into a repetitious clatter and I recognised the sound as the whirr of rotor blades. Then, back from the direction I'd come, a beam of light stabbed from the sky. The helicopter circled, hovering. It was a police chopper and it had located something of interest. I guessed it was maybe three miles away. Then the needle of light cut out, and the noise of the rotor blades became louder. I realised I was in trouble. Police helicopters carry infra-red heat detecting cameras. I knew that because I'd once done some consultancy work for Strathclyde police. I'd seen one in action. When the camera strayed over to where I was I'd be a glowing white figure, ablaze with body heat. I'd stand out like a snowman on Westminster Bridge. I'd be impossible to miss.

Think. Quickly. I went down the steep, short slope to the lochan, pulling off my rucksack as I went. I tore off my clothes, my boots. The coldness of the night hit my naked body like someone slapping it with an icy towel. I stuffed the rucksack and clothes into a dark gap between the rocks, then stepped into the lochan. The water was colder than ice, colder than anything imaginable. It was as intense as fire. I suddenly remembered news stories of people jumping into icy cold pools and suffering heart attacks. But that was in high summer. I was going from cold to colder. I was in up to my waist, my feet touching slimy rock. The chopper sounded like it was right overhead. It made a noise like a ship's engine room, an ear-splitting rhythmic din, the blades slashing the air. I sank down, holding my breath. I reached out and groped for weeds and miraculously found some. Such miracles always exist in thrillers. My fists tightened around the bunched fictive vegetation. I gripped on tight, anchoring myself below the surface, imagining how it felt.

Underwater, the noise of the helicopter seemed twice as intense. I imagined I was about to explode. My ears were bursting with noise, my lungs with fire. I could hold on no longer, and burst to the surface, gasping for breath. The chopper was almost exactly overhead. A huge beam of light probed the heather, maybe twenty metres away, casting a sudden glow over the lochan. I forced myself under again, scrabbling for the weed. Strangely, I could no longer feel the cold. My body felt weightless, completely numb. The only sensation I was aware of was the roaring in my ears. The water seemed to magnify the noise. It was like a physical sensation. Bands of noise passed through the water like waves, beating my eardrums. I broke the surface again, again gasping for narrative suspense. But something had changed. Everything was dark and silent.

I wondered if I'd passed out. Maybe I was dead, or dreaming. I was naked and wet, in a landscape that Dante might have imagined. My style had become lurid, extreme, desperate. The helicopter had gone. I heard its faint drone vanishing in the distance. I hauled myself out of the water and groped for my rucksack and clothes. Feeling returned and my whole body started shaking violently. I grabbed my T-shirt and used it as a towel, wiping myself dry. I finished off using my jumper. Luckily I had replacements in my rucksack. A good adventurer always blocks the loopholes. I put my clothes back on, still shivering uncontrollably. The two sodden garments I stuffed as far as I could into a rock fissure. I slipped the rucksack on and headed back up the slope. At the top I did a quick standing still jog, trying to get some warmth into my limbs. I'd have given anything at that moment for a slug of brandy. But someone had drunk it and the cupboard was bare. I made do instead with a half-price Australian red from Sainsbury's. I walked on, sipping the wine, still shivering in my mind. It was maybe half an hour later that a crag loomed out of the darkness on the laptop screen. In the starlight I could just make out a stubby spire of rock, rising out of the heather. Scooped out of the stone at its base, eroded by the course of a long-dead stream, was a low, curving space big enough to squeeze into. I tore off clumps of heather and scattered them on the rock as a makeshift mattress, and crawled in, dragging the rucksack with me as a pillow. I lay down to sleep.

I didn't sleep. The bitter cold fingered every part of me. Even my bones felt chilled. I wriggled to find a warm, comfortable position, never finding one, convincing myself that one more re-arrangement of my limbs might do the trick. I couldn't resist looking at my watch. A mistake. Time stretched itself out. Time moved with a slowness suffused with malice. I was being punished by it. Five minutes seemed like half an hour. In the end I gave up and just lay there, doing my best to rest. Eventually, somehow, without being aware of it, I slipped into a kind of frozen stupor. I came out of it to a world of whiteness. Everything had vanished. Baffled, I was once more in a landscape out of Dante. I started to think I was in one of those movies where the people are dead and don't realise it. Weird things happen, because it's a world of spectres and phantoms. Nothing has solidity – except the narrative.

My aching bladder said No, this is still the real world. I rolled sideways and stood up stiffly. My legs ached as if I'd run a marathon. I urinated against the rock face, and glanced at my watch. Five in the morning. The air smelled of the sea – a faint, fierce tang of salt and seaweed. Memories of a vulva. And I realised the whiteness was fog, not a gutter margin. The screech of a seagull told me what I'd already started to guess. I was very close to a realism coast. A thick sea fog had rolled in, enveloping the shoreline. I moved past the rock spire and almost once reached the plateau's edge. The land dropped sharply away into a foggy void. All I had to do was descend to the end of the paragraph, then turn right and walk until I reached the jetty and the parked Land Rover. There was a risk the police might be there ahead of me, but it seemed unlikely. An arrest would spoil the suspense. And last night's helicopter was a sign that the foot search had been called off. Even if they were setting off again now I'd still be ahead of them by a good margin. I started to make my way carefully down the page.

I heard the loch before I saw it. Visibility in the fog was about five metres. The sound of waves slapping on rock came to me several minutes before I reached the base of the slope and the ground levelled out. The beach consisted of a thin strip of grassland which dropped away on to rocks. Water came into view but the fog remained dense and I had no idea precisely where I was or how far I had to walk to reach the jetty for Achnamuirin. Only Ellis Sharp knew that – at least, I hoped he did. I sat down on a rock and rested. I was exhausted and cold and hungry. I knew I couldn't last very long without commas, end stops and a fresh supply of paragraphs. Twenty four hours at the most. After that I'd have to retreat to Mallaig and try my hand as a writer of magazine stories. Things didn't look good. I could see how this was all going to end. Genre fiction obeys its own iron laws. And in the eyes of a jury I was acting as guilty as hell. I was a man running from the law. Why would an innocent man do a thing like that? I stroked my jaw. Correction: an unshaven man was running from the law. Now I was even starting to *look* like a criminal, as well as *act* like one. And then something extraordinary happened. A door opened, and footsteps clicked on stone. And from somewhere close by me in the fog came the irresistible aroma of frying bacon.

The footsteps clicked closer and a woman in her thirties materialised in the mist. She was wearing a worn brown leather jacket over a black dress and top. The clicking was her stiletto heels. Her face was as white as the fog, accentuating the shocking contrast of her fiery red hair. She wore her hair cropped short, like a helmet jammed down over her head. She was scowling. She looked like someone who'd dragged on a jacket and stepped out from a party where she'd just had a row with her boyfriend.

When she saw me she gasped in shock, and her hand went over her mouth. Then she said, 'Who the fuck are you? What are you *doing* here?'

It was Quin. She didn't seem to know me at all. I was so far back inside time she'd evidently forgotten me. I reverted to the first draft of my story. I said: 'I'm sorry if I frightened you. I'm hopelessly lost. I spent last night up there.' I pointed back up the slope. 'I'm on a walking holiday with friends. We got separated up on the hills. The cloud came over without warning. Next thing it was night. I've been wandering around for hours. We're camping in Morar. Is that far?' The mixture of anger and surprise ebbed from her face. She thawed a little, then some more. Soon she was no more than a puddle, and after that a stain. After that all that was left to me was her books. I gazed at their covers with an infinite sense of sadness. I wanted to apologise for my style, for my old mistakes, but it was all too late for that. What's done is done, as mother used to say. But then time ran abruptly backwards, a hurricane sucked at my clothing and messed with my hair. I flinched and took hold of a stanchion which had risen out of nowhere. Glistening cobbles were all around me. I was reminded of Elm Hill in the rain.

Quin smiled. 'Sorry. You gave me rather a shock, just appearing out of nowhere. I heard noises last night. Distant shouting, and a helicopter. I guessed it must be some visiting genre fiction.' She hesitated a moment, then said: 'You'd better come with me. Have some breakfast. Clean yourself up.' 'That would be marvellous. I feel in a dreadful state, to be honest. I've been up all night. And I'm intolerably oppressed by banality.' I felt the words tumbling out of me. I was in a daze, a haze, a maze. Who was this woman, and where was she from? Who is any woman? Was there a house nearby?

'I'm Milena, by the way,' Quin said. 'As in Kafka biography.' There was something vaguely familiar about her. Like I'd once seen her at a party, or something. Seen her, but never talked to her. 'Hi,' I said. 'I'm Cliff Tollinger. I'm a character.' 'Come this way.' She stepped back into the mist and I followed. A spasm of pain ran through me as I stood up. I felt arthritic, heartbroken, old. I hurried to keep up with her, afraid that my angel of mercy might melt away as abruptly as she'd first appeared. Her stilettos clicked along a short flagstone path, then up something concrete constructed over some nouns. A huge shape loomed out of the mist, rising up into the sky. I saw that it was a paragraph. I wondered if it was the one I'd looked at through binoculars two days ago. 'Come in,' she said, pausing by a new sentence which led to an open door set at the base of the white curving wall. I followed her inside, and found myself in a big, open circular narrative structure. More nouns and verbs led away up to the top, curling round the interior of the walls. From an open door came that mouth-watering smell of bacon. I was reminded of *The Matrix*. The doorway opened on to a small, whitewashed kitchen. 'Shit,' she said. 'It's starting to burn.' On a gas stove an enormous, blackened frying pan was gently cooking an egg, two halves of tomato and some rashers of bacon. She pulled the pan away. 'Hungry?' 'I'm starving. I haven't had any verisimilitude for over two pages.' 'You poor thing. Here, you have this, I'll do some more. I'm not short of supplies. My dictionary is limitless.'

She gestured at a small wooden table. Just four words, in all their primitive simplicity. 'Tea?' 'Please. Milk, no sugar.' I removed my rucksack and put it against the wall, beside a big blue Calor Gaz cylinder. I cut myself and then I cut myself two slices of bread and butter. I tucked eagerly into the plateful of nouns and adjectives she set before me. Quin slipped off her leather jacket and put more nouns in the pan. 'So, how long are you up here for?' she asked. 'Just a few days,' I said. 'But in another way – forever.' I cited a certain sonnet. Outside, waves beat against the shore. A thought occurred to me, or so I thought. Like a ventriloquist's dummy I said: 'Say, do you have a phone? I really ought to call my friends. Tell them I'm safe.' My voice seemed shrill, even squeaky. 'Ah, big problem here, I'm afraid. Communication is impossible. This place is as dead as it gets. There's no landline and you can't get a signal on a mobile. There's no radio or TV either. The only contact with the outside world is D'eath the boatman. He calls from time to time. Otherwise it's a four hour walk to civilisation. There's no car here, of course. No road, either.' I listened impassively. I squeezed some more wrinkles into my corrugated brow. 'When did D'eath last call?' 'Just the other day. He won't be back for a while.' She smiled warily and flicked some water droplets off her breast.

'You're up very early,' I said, looking at my watch. 'In this place I go to sleep very early and I get up very early,' she explained. 'Morning's when I'm sharpest. The same's true for Sharp, you know.' She added: 'I do my best stuff at dawn.' She multiplied her text and smiled. 'After that it's downhill all the way. Like birth. Or the aftermath of a grand passion.' She smiled again, having exhausted her repertoire of expressions. 'Sometimes I walk out and look at the loch. I was doing that just now. I get mentally blocked, so I walk down the steps and admire the scenery. It's soothing. I see things. Seals. Gulls. Fragments of text.' 'And what are you working on now?' I asked. She had not said what her 'stuff' was, but of course I knew. *The Unmapped Country*. Her smile faded. 'I never discuss my work until it's finished,' she said. Her voice was iron. Beneath it lay paper coated in black markings. The waves slapped stupidly against the shoreline. The sound of a motor broke through the silent landscape and we both stopped talking. I wondered if it

Quin Again

was the helicopter. But the motor sounded different. Quin picked up a convenient pair of binoculars from a convenient shelf and went to a conventional and rather plain door to look out. I followed her and looked over her shoulder. I realised Quin was physically smaller than I remembered her. The fog had melted away, leaving just a few ghostly strands adrift in the centre of the sea loch. From the great sweep of sea to the west a white boat was approaching. 'It's the police,' she said. 'They're probably looking for a body. There was a woman swam out to sea last week. She never returned.'

'They're here for me,' I said. 'You must hide me, please. Please believe me when I tell you that I'm an innocent man. Don't believe what they say about me. It isn't true. If you have seen the films of Alfred Hitchcock you must believe me.' Quin looked looked suddenly bewildered. 'Come with me,' she said. She led me past the kitchen to a door at the back. It resembled a prison cell. The door was practically medieval, made of wood studded with iron bolts. At the top there was a hatch with bars. Inside it was gloomy and windowless. 'It's an old store room. There's a lot of old lighthouse stuff in it, waiting to be taken away. Someone was supposed to remove it before I moved in, but they never did. I'll lock the door and pretend I don't have a key. You can hide under an old tarpaulin, or something. Go on!' She pushed me in, and turned the huge key in the lock. Her stilettos clicked away into the distance. I suddenly remembered all kinds of things. My rucksack lying in the kitchen. The two plates on the table, indicating that she had a visitor. But it was already too late to start yelling at her: the noise of the boat's engine echoed through the lighthouse interior.

My eyes adjusted to the darkness. I knew the darkness might last for decades. The room went back about five metres. In the gloom I could make out a dozen packing cases, four life belts, some red fire buckets (still containing sand), a folded tarpaulin and bits and pieces of miscellaneous clutter including a pair of Wellington boots. I dragged out the tarpaulin, which was heavier than I expected. I hauled it into the corner of the room which was just to the right of the door. Already I could hear a male voice and the sound of heavy footsteps clattering on stone flagstones. I crawled under the tarpaulin. It smelled of diesel fuel. I pulled it over my head. I lay still and waited.A muffled conversation. Footsteps. A man's voice saying, 'If you don't mind, we'd like to take a look around.' The sound of several people making their way up the curving stairs. Dim, distant voices; echoing. Silence. All the detritus of a suspense narrative.

Then the footsteps returning and more conversation. The footsteps coming up to the room in which I was hiding. Someone turning the knob, pushing to open the door.

Quin saying: 'I don't have a key to this room. It's kept locked. It's full of stuff to do with the lighthouse. Someone is supposed to be coming over from Mallaig to clear it out. He couldn't possibly be in there.' Conversation by the hatch. I could almost feel the police eyes scanning the gloomy interior like searchlights. I kept absolutely still. I didn't think the tarpaulin was even visible from the hatch but I didn't want to give myself away if it was. Footsteps, going away. The conversation growing fainter.

Silence. The minutes passed. Then the sound of a

motor starting. The boat chugged away into the distance. Click, click, click. Quin came back. She looked through the bars of the hatch. 'They've gone,' she said. 'Thanks for that.' 'They said they'd come back tomorrow.' I waited for the sound of the key turning in the lock. Instead she just looked at me. 'The police think you're so dangerous they wanted me to leave on the boat with them. I told them it was out of the question. They said they'd come back tomorrow. Just to make sure I was safe. I think they meant, just to make sure I was still *alive*.' The dead woman's words kept repeating in my skull. Other words hammered at the walls of my story. My Love, my Love, my Love, I am so full of your presence that my eyes keep brimming over and I hear your voice in my ears and feel your hands on my body and all the words I say express only a minute fraction of what I feel.

'I'm sorry. I couldn't tell you I make things up. There just wasn't time. We'd only just met. Can I come out now, please?' She looked sad. 'I'm sorry. I can't take that risk.' 'If you think I'm a postmodernist, why didn't you tell the police?' 'I don't know. I suppose I believed what you said. About being realistic. It was only after I told them you weren't here that they told me you were an ontological subversive. I felt such a fool. I could hardly say, well, actually, he is here. And anyway I feel all mixed up. Maybe they're wrong, maybe they're not. I don't know. I need a hot shot of intertextuality. That would be cool. Sorry. I feel very, very confused. I'm going to have you leave you here. For the moment. I can't let you loose. You might start undreaming things, then where would we be?'

Soon I could hear the sound of a kettle being filled. Sounds travelled inside the lighthouse; it was like a great echo chamber. I sat down with my back to the wall and waited. I didn't have to wait very long. About ten minutes later she came storming back. 'What,' she shouted, 'is the meaning of *this*?' She waved a book at me through the bars. It was a skinny paperback. *Passages.* It was the Dalkey Archive edition of 2003. 'This,' she said. 'I found it in your rucksack. What sort of game are you playing, Tollinger?' 'A postmodern one, I suppose,' I whispered. My voice was drowned by the crash of water against a pier. 'You came here deliberately, didn't you?' 'Only in my mind.' I said: 'I can explain.' But a whole slice of the last draft seemed to have been deleted and I realised I was lost.

I told her everything I could remember. Scraps, fragments, rags. I slumped in the darkness and told stories. I ran the movie of my life. I identified the soundtrack. I mentioned the identity parade. I gave her the whole caboodle. Right down to the walk along the Morar path. She listened in silence. She went away. She returned. I could smell coffee. I went on with my story. I'd been carrying everything around bottled up inside me for too long. I wanted to confess. She gave me a thin smile. I wondered if I could make it obese. Silence. Time's passage. She said at last: 'How in hell am I supposed to know what's true and what isn't?' 'Are you going to turn me in?' 'I haven't decided.' 'And what's going to make you decide one way or the other?' 'I've really no idea. Time, maybe.' She went away. Exhaustion hit me like a needle full of anaesthetic. I fell asleep at once.

When I woke the room seemed darker. I looked at my watch and realised why. I'd been asleep for almost ten hours. It was night. The adjectives were sparse. I peered out through the hatch. A single bare bulb burned, giving a bleak, prison-like tinge to the whitewashed brick walls. Quin was asleep in the corridor. She'd dragged an armchair from somewhere and was curled up in it. Her head rested on her right hand, which lay curled back against the back of the chair, the arm bent back beside her breast. She looked pale and doll-like. 'I'm sure this is against the Geneva Convention,' I said. Quin managed a wintry smile, then an autumnal one. 'I'll see what I can do.' Entire sentences had been cut out. Others had been messed around with. She went silently from view. A raised hand, a slight swirl of water, some bubbles. The departure gate at the terminal. Evidently she'd given up on the stilettos. She came back with ---- -------------, then she sloped off. Something clattered in the cluttered kitchen. I heard her swear. She was on edge. I set it aside. I went back to the packing cases. The third one contained something dark and floppy. It smelled of rubber. As I hauled it out I saw loops. There was a small plastic tube with a cap protruding from the skin of the object. There was something underneath the floppy, folded mass. A hand pump. It was a small one-character rubber dinghy. All I needed was (i) to inflate it, and (ii) to get out of my locked room. I got to work with the pump. I had it half-inflated when Quin came back with a tray. 'Look,' I said, pointing. 'Our problems are over. With this I can paddle away into the sunset. Just take these chains from my heart and set me free. I can take it on the chin if I must. Soon I'll soon be out of your hair. Any ketchup?' 'Fuck off,' she said. Then she dropped two bananas through the bars and said: 'Your pudding.' Silence. And then a door slamming shut far away. And the echoing crash of a metal bolt sliding into place. And the slow soft slither of an unzipped banana.

I killed time by inflating the dinghy. Light-headed, I slept and dreamed of a slim novella. It had a blue cover and a shimmery title. *Quin Again Woke* was the title. As for the dinghy. It was pitifully small but the island wasn't too far offshore. I slept, but only fitfully. A hermaphrodite chased me along a collapsing bridge. A rabbit attempted to gnaw my right ear. A whirlpool formed in my tomato soup, then winked at me. Milena assaulted my heart repeatedly with a sledgehammer. The pallbearers dropped my coffin and I rolled across the road in a swirl of white sheeting. Quin was thumping on the door. She returned ten minutes later and thumped again. She looked flushed, a little dazed. 'An egg,' she said, passing me one. 'May I take the dinghy?' I said. 'I wouldn't want it any other way.' She came back when I was ready to go. In her sweet hand she held a gun. It wasn't a conventional gun. It was bigger and fatter and bore a vague resemblance to a water pistol. 'This thing shoots distress flares. At point blank range it can do you a lot of damage. If you were hit in the face it would blind you. It might even kill you.'

I did exactly what the narrative conventions demanded. I projected, I displaced, I invented. I wrapped the mess up like a lump of bloodied and bleeding meat. I mopped up the drips. I cut away the fat. I shaped it. I made a story. Fiction frothed and fizzed in the embers. Then smoke gets in your eyes. Looking at the fierce, unhappy, intense expression on her face I didn't doubt her reality. She was transparent and I never realised. She seemed nervy and ill-at-ease and tangible. She unlocked the fictitious door and stepped back. I came out, holding the dinghy and its paddles. None of this happened. Everything had become desperate and absurd. The props were lightweight but cumbersome to write. I walked slowly to the lobby and out of the lighthouse, and back down the steps which I'd imagined walking up twenty-four hours earlier. I strained my ears for the sound of the police boat coming back. Nothing – just the faraway screeching of some gulls. The endless slap of waves on Brighton beach. The tide curdling in the mud estuary. The long footbridge at Shoreham-by-Sea, where I walked as a child. The bridge lined with painted advertisements, long gone, which seem enormous.

It was probably far too early in the morning for what was inevitable. The sun was still invisible behind the mountains. A thin brilliance outlined their summits but the sky was grey. Quin had put my rucksack on the quayside. All I had to do was go down a flight of worn, stained steps and lower the dinghy into the water. I tied it to a rusty iron ring and came back for the paddles and the rucksack. She kept her distance from me, levelling the flare pistol at me in a way that made me nervous. 'Can't you put that thing down now?' I said. 'You might fire it accidentally.' She lowered it slightly, so that it pointed at the ground about half way between us. I climbed into the dinghy and sat there. She came to the top of the steps and looked down at me. 'What will you say to the police when they come to see if you're alright? Are you going to tell them about me?' 'What police?' she said. 'What you? I've never met you.' 'I suppose that's true. By the way, I meant to ask. What's the new book about?' 'Something coming to an end,' she said tersely. 'Now just *go*, will you. Fuck off. Now!' She raised the flare pistol, aimed it at my face. 'Okay, stay cool! I'm going!'

I pushed off with the paddle. I turned a circle and brought the dinghy crashing against the quay wall. In my mind I pushed off again and started to get the hang of how paddling must be. Not that it was entirely imaginary. There were those sunny days in the pool at Burton Bradstock. I felt the narrative pressing down. In a series of zigzags, I headed away from the quayside. I brought the dinghy parallel with the shoreline, and, staying about ten metres offshore, I started propelling myself due east. When Quin was about fifty metres away I rested the paddles on the floor of the dinghy and shouted, 'Thanks for everything! Love you!' I blew her a kiss. She made no response but just stayed there, silent, immobile, watching, stiff as a cemetery angel. The rising sun caught the glass at the top of the lighthouse, throwing back a blinding sheet of fire. I lowered my gaze. I rowed on, and round a small headland, and she disappeared from the text.

I kept paddling for an hour, hugging the verbs and nouns. I calculated that if the police boat or the helicopter re-appeared I'd hear them before I saw them and have time to get ashore with the dinghy and hide. It was lightweight and black and from a distance would look like just another rock in the landscape. This was the kind of thing that happened in adventure stories. I suppose I'd never really freed myself from *The Thirty-Nine Steps*. Staying just a few metres from the shore also made it less likely that I could be seen by anyone on the hills above. The shoreline looped from promontory to promontory in a sequence of miniature bays, and each bay was more or less hidden from view, except to someone standing on the steeply rising ground directly above. Scotland was perfect for this kind of hokum.

Quin Again

The imaginary island of Achnamuirin came into view. Patches of sea mist drifted slowly over it, lending it an enchanted quality. I stayed inshore, continuing until I reached the spot where I'd first emerged from the valley path two days earlier. Fifteen minutes later I was at the jetty. I stepped out on to the shore, hauling the dinghy after me. I found a suitable hiding place under some nearby ferns. I glanced inside the garage and saw that the Land Rover was still parked there. Taking the rucksack with me I walked a little way along the rocky beach to stretch my legs. A bunch of midges swarmed in a tiny cloud at treetop height. The sun was now high in the sky, Loch Nevis a Mediterranean blue. I sank down into some ferns, tucked the rucksack under my head, and closed my eyes. Warmth touched my face, my clothes. A wild bee came droning by. The genre felt deliciously soothing and safe. I dozed off, a little fuddled by plot and language.

I didn't hear the ----. What woke me was the sound of the ---- being ---- out of the ----, and away up the ----. At the same time the ---- into life, and the ----- went ---- back across the ---- to the ----. I let two minutes pass, then cautiously ---- my ---- above the ----. The ---- was already some distance from the ----, leaving a ---- behind it. The engine of the ---- faded somewhere in the ---- above me. I took out the ---- and ---- the ----. A solitary person at the controls; a splash of ---- hair. Probably the ---- woman I'd seen before. Which meant someone else was ----. The ---- reached the ---- at the ---- and ----out of ----. Now seemed as good a time as any to make the ----. I guessed the ---- was headed for Mallaig. That meant I had a couple of hours at the very least to ---- across to the ---- undisturbed. I decided to go back to the clump of ferns where I'd hidden the noun. Moments later I heard the sound of a ---- approaching. I couldn't understand why the ---- was ---- so soon. Something white ---- between the trees above me and I realised it wasn't ----. It ---- by the ---- and I heard ----, then the crackle of ----. 'It's like a bloody jungle!' a voice ----. 'Over here!' someone ----, further away. I guessed they'd ---- the ----. The ---- started ----.

I lay in the shadow of everything, not moving. An ant approached my right hand, then scampered across it. In the distance nouns and verbs and adjectives crashed noisily through the frenetic plot. I waited. When all was silent once again I crept back towards a convenient noun. Everyone had gone. The days were crushed and broken on the far side. A trail of trodden down lives led off alongside the shore. I guessed what had happened. Love had been here. It would lead my pursuers back to the pathway alongside Loch Morar. I'd had enough. I waded into the water. It felt unpleasantly cold for August. I swam out to sea. The hillside here, though still densely forested, rose steeply to the barren, windswept wastes. I trod water and examined two imaginary volumes of verse. The first was titled *Ceremony of Ghosts*, the second *A Street Off Pico*. It wasn't the day for reading poetry. I wasn't sure there ever would be such a day. I let the books slip away and sink.

Time passed. It killed me. Insects flew by. The night is long. The island is a lump of darkness set in a paler darkness. Water slaps me. The wind is getting up. I was hoping I might see a light shining on Quin's island, to guide me. No such luck. The south side of the island seems barren and forbidding. The dispiriting thought occurs to me that Quin isn't there, or if she is she won't see me. There's only one way to find out. I press on, carving through the water. The wind starts to push me off course, taking me back to the past. I correct my direction and redouble my efforts, trying to speed up. I'm perhaps only fifty yards away from the shore, but already it seems a vast distance back to the mainland. In the twilight a strange optical illusion occurs. It's as if the island is a ship and is starting to move. It's as if Quin was directly ahead of me and now she's drawn up its anchor and is setting sail. The island is starting to turn on its axis.

And now the current is sucking me past the island and out past the headland. For the first time I begin to feel that I'm in real danger. This part of the narrative seems to be drawing to a close, and then I'll be gone. The sea, like life generally, seems to be getting rougher. Water splatters across my face. There's a glimmer of phosphorescence in the font. A pool of water forms at the end of the tale, slopping to and fro. The faint glow there is suggestive of an explanation. My corruptible heart is on fire with stars. These stars shimmer and sparkle with a brilliance I've never seen before. And now I'm growing tired, very tired. I looked round for the lights on the pier. It takes time to locate them. An eternity. There can be no doubt, now. I am being swept out to the end of things. I've lost all sense of who I am and who she is, Quin. A dark mass looms. When I see a solution I paddle towards it, hoping for the comfort of an explanation. But each time the current sweeps me on. More time passes. I look at my bedside clock and see it is two in the morning. I need to piss. The only consolation is that eventually, finally, the dawn will come, and this paragraph will be over. My mind wanders. I start thinking of the old days.

I wander down corridors, listening to voices and music. I stand on a sunlit balcony. A familiar old song is playing and I strain to recognise it. Its name is on the tip of my tongue. The words start to form, then fall away, snapped off by the sound of an engine. I glance up and see ahead of me a white, bobbing light. It floats just above the surface of the water. Behind it is a blazing window and the outline of a dark figure.

It's getting closer all the time, the thing that is getting closer all the time, the person who is getting closer all the time. It's coming to rescue me. Thoughts which evaporate as I reach the opposite conclusion. I am just a dark nothing in a dark sea, too low and tiny to be picked up on any vessel's radar. I am sodden and inert. I am done for. My lungs slop with salt water, my eyes are that angel's. Frantically I revert to the first draft of my banal escapist adventure text. I snatched up the paddles and began thrashing the water, to get out of the path of this monster. The noise of the engine was now as loud as if I'd been on board. I could see the man in the boathouse. He had one hand on the wheel; the other was holding a mug. He seemed to be staring straight at me. As I watched, he tweaked the wheel slightly, bringing it back on course to hit me full on. I paddled wildly, knowing I wasn't going to make it.

It surged at me like Moby-Dick, a great white whale parting the seas with massive rhetoric. The white sharp bow of the craft came at me like a gigantic powerful simile. It was preceded by a tidal wave of roaring foam, which contemptuously flipped the clichés up and away. The side of the ship smacked against the air-swollen rubber, which contracted like flesh at the blow. The crossbeam shuddered. Its spasms transmitted themselves up my legs. The dinghy went hurling away to the side, and the boat roared by. A giant number flashed by, painted on the side. I glimpsed a cluster of dimly lit aerials. The ship was a trawler. It at once brought to mind a five shilling Panther and a cover design by Jack Larkin, with photography by KR.

My text crashed down amid its boiling wake, spun round once, and was suddenly at peace again, alone on a suddenly calm noun. The white whale churned noisily away into the distance. After about ten minutes it suddenly disappeared behind an invisible headland. I reached down for more adjectives but they'd gone. They must have been washed or knocked overboard by the force of the impact. I held my head between my hands. It made a change from my penis. There was nothing I could do now but drift and go where the narrative took me. I felt drained of all energy and will power. I knew now I was just a character, caught up in some pomo shenanigans. I would have liked to lie down and get some rest but the floor of the dinghy was awash with water. My rucksack was sodden and ruined. Life's a bugger. I sat and ached. I yawned. Somehow, in the end, I dozed.

I kept waking up. That didn't help. Unconscious states may be preferable. I have colourful dreams. I hold conversations with my favourite singers. They find me interesting. They listen, rapt. In dreams you never fart. It seems to be bitterly cold. I'm shivering. I have a landscape report for you. The sky is still lurid with great swathes of flashing stars. I doze off again. An interesting word: *doze*. I wake, I doze again. I frequently jot down interesting words. It was always night and then, unexpectedly, I woke, and everything around me was white and fluffy and drifting.

It was dawn but a dense sea fog had swept over everything. I could see about five yards but no further. I was in a world of perfect silence. The surface flat calm. I wondered where I was, and hoped it was not Shoreham harbour. If I'd drifted past Skye in the night I was done for. I looked at my watch. It was midnight. I tried to work out if anything was moving, but it was hard to tell. I sat and shivered and waited. I had nothing else to do. Time passed. I heard a solitary splash nearby, as if someone had dropped a rock into the water. Then silence. Anything would be better than this.

I knew I should have given myself up to the cops when I had the chance. They would have arrested me and kept me safely locked up in a realistic prison cell. Structure would have surrounded my limited mobility. I would have been safe and comfortable. They had nothing on me. Circumstances might look bad but I was an innocent man. I would have been bored, yet comfortable. Better to have taken my chance in front of a jury than end up like this. I was shivering with more than just cold now. I stared anxiously around me. The past tense was consoling. It seemed to indicate that I had eventually moved beyond this horror. It seemed to hint that I was now able to look back from somewhere safer. A place from where I could speak in a calm voice of what had occurred.

A dark wave rises gently up and passes over me. Icy salt water soaks my hair and chokes my nostrils and mouth. I spit it out, gasping for air. To my horror everything swings into the present tense. Sharp shapes drift by on the vast waters. A shark's fin? The detritus of a sunken ship? A clutter of interpolations and bifurcations, dangerously adrift? The style is sleek as varnish. A writer might drown out here and never be seen again. A shark's fin? I remember seeing *Jaws* in Ottawa with Milena. Snow lay all about, deep and crisp and even. And now hear the sound of waves slapping against rocks. A dark mass looms out of the mist. Another story takes shape. My feet touch rock. I wade the last two yards to a narrow strip of pebbled text. When I look back everything has gone. All I can imagine is a rag of dark rubber, drifting to and fro in the waves. I wonder where I was, where I am, where I will be. The next paragraph looks too smooth and steep to climb, so I set off in another direction.

The mist is thinning fast. A yellow aura in the sky shows where the sun is beginning to burn through. I am too exposed where I am. I am giving too much of my self away. Selves. Another ten minutes, and I will find a little space to hide. Pine trees, a cooing dove, the props of a tired imagination. A climate of thin sunshine. A cold dark gully would be good. A trench. Perhaps a space beneath the walkway. I designed this deleted building: I know all the best places to hide. I crouch in a cold, dark pit of language, hearing the clatter go by above me. The clatter becomes my pitiful heart, my pulse. It always was. All my pursuers are imaginary. I shall stay here for a little while and think things over. What to do, where to go next. I shall stay in this draft for months, doing other things. The story disintegrates at this point. I can take it up at a later date. Take it up and go on. Across the river and into the trees and all what happens next.

Quin reaches out her hands. Her eyes are wet. Tollinger grips her frail body. Now they are dancing, though they never danced before. Now they are dancing in an empty room. There is music in that empty room. Someone is singing, repeating the word September. They dance at the edge of the cliff, they share their reminiscences, they tumble and fall. A thump, a thud, a heartbeat, and Tollinger wakes in a white empty room. See the lighthouse in the distance, tangible as any computer-generated image. At the quayside the motor boat is waiting. The plot is more or less over. The cops know Tollinger didn't do whatever it was he was supposed to have done. Quips and male badinage relax the accumulated tension. Quin is standing there in the doorway. There's a tiny smile on her face. Tollinger is forgiven everything. The cops are long gone. There's just the two of them now. Water slops against the dark wall.

Quin Again

Waves break on the shoreline. Now she has a silver car key in her hand. They get into the car to go where lovers go. 'Drive faster, damn you,' Tollinger cries. 'Faster.' The road winds up the hillside and goes over the crest. The white sky looks as if it is about to split in two. A gash of incandescence absorbs them.

3: Texts

DO I HAVE ANY rights where the State is concerned? Not really, no. They like to pretend I do, but I don't. Under the text and terms of the Mental Health Act I am legally entitled to a leaflet outlining my rights according to the Section under which I have been detained. There are other leaflets. There are many leaflets. We, the persistently perturbed, battle our way bravely forwards through a blizzard of words. Advice patters down like an unending shower of soft excrement (the warm malleable variety which I enjoy daubing my walls with). Information is available regarding the care which is available under the relevant Section Order. Meantime, out there in the sane world, the ice caps melt and the sea level rises. Out there the trade in bombs, bullets, restraints and repression is brisk. Exceptionally brisk. Out there the clinically sane manoeuvre their way recklessly around densely populated urban areas in lethal bubbles of toxic steel, trailing corpses and broken bones. There are contacts if you have any questions. Other information is available pertaining to guardianship, supervised discharge or hospital orders with restrictions. Information, advice, words, treacle, sedation, sedation, sedation. The sane have their bestsellers. They have their must-see movies. They have their sporting spectacles and celebrity gossip.

Quin Again

I have half a mind. It has been suggested I should stop there, but I'll continue. I have half a mind to go to the railway station in the next town and ask for a ticket to the Washington Avenue Bridge in Minneapolis. One-way, obviously.

In London I asked Jacques Roubaud to sign my copy of *The Great Fire of London*, which he did. I then turned the book over. I pointed out to him that Foyles had experienced a difficulty in categorising his book. Although I had located his book under FICTION the bookseller had identified it as *Category: – Unknown*. Roubaud laughed. He was delighted by this. 'So would you define it as a novel?' I enquired. His response was fierce. 'No, it is not a novel!' he retorted, very emphatically.

This was some time before I encountered the term biofiction.

White feathers in the snow. Paper scraps. I don't know how much longer I have. We have. How long this can last. I am living comfortably at the top of this old house, safe from the rising waters. I stand on my balcony. I stare at the lighthouse. I go inside again, lashed by solitude. When I went out today, I had to turn back. Flood water had cut off both ends of the street. A NO ENTRY sign seemed to float on the water surface like a red ball. A woman stared from an upstairs window. It wasn't Quin.

And a chopper hovered. The sky was as grey as my mind. None of this existed. It was old news. The footage rolled through the boredom of my morning.

Sometimes I knew I was on the island; sometimes I thought I was in the insane asylum; sometimes I was the director of the insane asylum.

I always preferred the end of the original *Blade Runner* to the director's cut.

Twenty-eight days without a drink. Difficult beyond words at times...

W & G FOYLE

9 781564 783967

14/03/2008

ISBN : 9781564783967 7.99
TITLE: GREAT FIRE OF LONDON
CAT: - Unknown

All wires twist and form knots. This I have noticed. The white wire of the white dehumidifier wraps itself around the white wire of the white oscillating fan. A second knot joins the first knot. Soon it requires great effort to detach them. The wires are hard-wired to create difficulties. This I have noticed.

'Too long in one town, Nelly.'

And still through the hawthorn blows the cold wind.

Brightening skies. Odd spots of drizzle possible.

Quin Again

INTERRUPTER: Is it all going to be as formless as this?
CHAIRMAN: Yes.

Miss Quin has relied on her extraordinary gift for language to salvage people who, I am afraid, are beyond salvation.

Spilt wisdom. I have filled many pages now. When I went to pull down the blind in the extension a quick black shape moved against the window against the night a moth I did not know if it was in the garden or in the room I decided it was outside but later when I closed my eyes I heard it fluttering in that dirty bedroom on the third floor of my mind.

Pessimism of the intellect. Optimism of the will.

That hot day I insisted we walk to the Via Gramsci, so that I could take a photograph. Just along from Lingomare Dante. That hot day I filmed you walking across London Bridge. That hot day you slipped off your floral knickers amid the sand dunes and I surreptitiously photographed you.

It isn't simply ad nauseam, *but beyond that into pure tedium.*

'My life is full of diaries.'

Cockadoodledoo!

That Shelby Lynn song.

And to make matters worse, it is derrière garde *literary, with run-on sentences and all.*

After you left, the balloons from your birthday hung around the house. It did not at first seem decent to take them down. But today all that is ended. I am releasing them into the wild. I cut them down, one by one. They were blue, white, red, orange, green. I took them one by one into the garden and threw them up into the air. The current lifted them into the sky. Up, up, up, they went, soaring towards the clouds. They blew south and vanished. Soon they would fade past the eyes of surprised rescue workers, passing like painted birds.

Bemusing to the point of complete incoherence, it invites no more than intellectual befuddlement.

All lies. Not a single balloon achieved lift-off. One by one they dropped to the ground. One limped to the nearest rose and burst. The others huddled like sheep.

Quin Again

The thing is still physically a book, we must still turn over its pages, we still have to remember from one page to the next what has accumulated. The effort of doing so through the thickets of frustration that the method and layout interpose is too much, and draws fatal attention to the powerful underlying humorlessness of the whole thing.

Not true either. They lay still. One or two then rolled around, as if half alive. I left them and went inside. The next day they were still there. It was a fortnight before they were gone.

And soon, if I need them, I can summon throngs of characters, and the little chains of events, and the immortal moments.

All lies. There was no birthday, there were no balloons. I cannot remember your birthday. Even the colour of your eyes is gone.

```
<object        width="425"         height="344"><param
name="movie"value="http://www.youtube.com/v/mT
arJoOp7W8&hl=en&fs=1"></param><paramname="a
llowFullScreen"value="true"></param><paramname=
"allowscriptaccess"value="always"></param><embeds
rc="http://www.youtube.com/v/mTarJoOp7W8&hl=e
n&fs=1"type="application/x-shockwave-flash"allow
scriptaccess="always"allowfullscreen="true"width="42
5" height="344"></embed></object>
```

Call your lovers from the stage of death.

It seems once again to be very, very hot. Soon the flying ants will creep out of the cracks and crawl around, dragging their folded, listless wings. Can't remember what minatory means. Or lapidary. Oppressed by the monosyllables of that ridiculous grandfather clock.

'Mr Alfau is in Miami.'

My teeth ache for you.

Eureka!

'It was so wonderful, once upon a time.' Says the alcoholic wife.

The trees are burning in your promised.

What is your occupation on this planet?

Land. Words. Are all. I have. Once more you open. The door. Someone left the cake out. In the rain. I want you. Send me dead flowers. In the morning. Fuck. Off.

I wake with thee and sleep with thee
And yet thou art not there.

I walked very slowly. The house seemed unending. I warn you that some of the ghosts are slightly monstrous.

'Chug-a-lug, Donna.'

And all the mornings of that year.

Quin Again

And all the mornings of that year.

Once, forty years ago, I tried to sleep with seductive Sylvia. She pushed me away. I am not ready for you yet, clumsy boy, she said. So I bandaged up my bruised wrists and spat out the sour residue of the pills and opened the door and walked down the corridor and out into the cold night air. The twinkly stars urged me to walk on. They promised shining galaxies and mystery. They pricked me with their piercing light. My lungs burned with cold.

What chance has Vulcan against Roberts & Co., Jupiter against the lightning-rod and Hermes against the Crédit Mobilier?

Something that happened last week: I went to Sainsbury's and bought some groceries. At the check-out I inserted my Delta card to pay for my groceries. I asked for thirty pounds cashback. I pressed four digits on the machine to give it my PIN number. The checkout woman shook her head. I am sorry, she said. It won't accept it. Since I had obviously slipped up with my PIN number I very carefully pressed the soft green buttons again. I am sorry, she said. It still won't take it. In that case I will pay with my Visa card, I said. I pressed four digits on the machine. A different four digits, obviously. That goes without saying. But if it goes without saying why did I say it? Because in one hundred years no reader will understand the details of this primitive financial transaction. Except that in one hundred years' time there will be no readers. Every student of Catastrophysics knows that. And you know what! My Visa card was accepted. But I was not allowed any cashback because you can only get cashback with a Delta card. I have never understood why but it is one of The Rules of the Bank. I expect there is a form I could fill in and I would be able to get cashback with a Visa card. But if there is one I shall never fill it in. I can't be bothered. While all this was going on I glanced at my rejected Delta card. Its rejection had stirred a memory. I remembered now I had had a letter from the bank a couple of weeks earlier. When I looked at the card I realised that it had expired two days earlier. I had a new card and I had forgotten all about it. It was still sitting there at home, waiting for me to remove it from its paper holder. 'Mystery solved!' I grinned at the checkout woman. 'My card expired!' She beamed back. Now she knew that I was not a fraudster, a thief or an Al-Qaeda operative! 'There's always a simple explanation!' she said.

Today I was standing in line when the check-out woman shouted: 'Trace, I need a void!'

And now all these years later I think I am ready to sleep with Elizabeth Smart. She is not too far away.

That's for my full life and all the women I want!'

I shall not imagine it, where all this is leading.

À bas les cadences infernales!

We were as close to Cape Wrath as we would ever be. You stopped the car and ran off across the wet sands. I think of you at that moment, Quin. About to return to the waters from which you came.

Quin Again

You were happy, happy, happy. You were oblivious to how I was about to smash that happiness. I was oblivious to how you were about to smash my happiness.

That graveyard? We both could have died then and there. Sang Joan of Arc after she sprang free from the fire and began a new career as an acrobat in a travelling circus.

Quin can write well; but in this piece of self-gratification she promulgates nothing more than the work of an artist at the end of her tether.

A scene in the biopic goes like this. We are on the beach. It is December and night has fallen. We have driven thirty miles to get here. Vee is wearing her big old fur coat. The tide is out. Hand in hand we walk slowly across the empty dark gleaming sands to that distant place where the waves go to die. Vee's gorgeous dark hair falls to her waist. A dense mist begins to drift in from the sea. Far behind us, by the shuttered funfair, a line of plastic palm trees is rattling frantically in the gust. And in the end all I can do is embrace her and kiss her and hold her very tightly and with a muddy, banging heart say all that is left to say.

I am done with words.

4: Cocusa

ALL HERE IS BLUE. Because here in Cocusa the only books permitted to be published or possessed are those with blue covers. Some form of rigour is necessary to someone in my imperial predicament.

An anecdote. Although now I adhere very strictly to blue this was not always the case. For a long time I preferred the fade-to-black-and-white version. In the first part of the film Geum-ja wears a blue coat. This is switched to a black leather coat at the end. And the walls of the prison and Geum-ja's bedroom are coloured. But the walls of the school are grey.

'What? Are you here too?' I had just gone round the bend when I saw him. I said these words to a young man on Gone West Street. He was selling the paper *Insurrectionary Proletarian*. Or rather, not selling the paper. People went by, ignoring him. Nobody wanted to think of themselves as proletarian. It degraded their sense of self. He kept up a brave cry against the empire and the emperor of Cocusa and the spore. But the people did not respond. He was startled when I went up to him. He didn't have a clue who I was. 'I didn't know you still existed,' I said. 'I thought you were finished.' My tone was friendly, even charming. 'No, we are still here,' he replied. 'There are still some of us left.' He smiled nervously. I could see he was afraid of the secret police. I bought a copy out of curiosity and walked away with my paper, hiding it quickly under my coat, as if it were pornography. It would not do for the emperor to be seen with such trash. At the corner I looked back. A police car had pulled up alongside the paper seller. Two officers stood talking to him. Then one of the cops took his arm and guided him into the car, which was driven away. I knew at once he would vanish from the narrative and never be heard of again. This is how things are in Cocusa. This is how things will always be.

Cocusa! The Brontë brats had their Gondal and their Angria. *Moi* – I have complete control of the empire of Cocusa. If I say it is raining in Cocusa, it rains. Here in Cocusa our language is different to yours. Take this, for example: R̂Ψ]¶ ʾÀ¿*ﻼﻜﻫ ‼‡ Ω'ψ'🜨 ʾI φ̰ p̳ ⊥ ῦ ώ K̂ ő ﬀ̱ 🙰Ж ز Ә χǓ꜀Ɔᴡ̃ضᵛꭓ. This translates as 'Tollinger loves Quin'. Be grateful that this entire text has been translated for you out of the original difficult Cocusan. But some sentiments are untranslatable. I have never been able to forget Quin. I still see her name in books. Her name pierces me like a knife.

Look! Something has passed across the wet sand, leaving huge furrows. Let me explain. I woke at five and was unable to get back to sleep, so I dressed and went down to the beach. And there I saw these enormous enigmatic marks. It must have occurred during the night, what it was that occurred. Just after the high tide's ebb. I counted over thirty furrows before the statistic began to seem pointless and I gave up. Metal had surely cut these monstrous grooves. Temporary scars, which the turning tide would soon heal. I followed the churned sand to where it all began. The derelict fairground had gone. It had evidently decided to crawl into the ocean and not return. I stared at the patterns of dead earth. That oval was where the dodgems had been. Over there had been the hall of crazy mirrors. The whirling merry-go-round had shed some coloured bulbs on its departure. They lay immaculate on the dark flat soil, in the company of broken bolts. Editor's footnote: *This occurred in Cocusa.*

A hot silky night under the stars! Cocusa is wonderful at this time of year. This would once have been delicious, in my lusty twenties. In my time of desire and enchantment. Time of candlelight and fondue for two and a double fuck on a broad bed. Time of passion and promises, before the spiders and the rats appeared. And now the air is filled with particulates which would kill me if I lived long enough, which I won't.

Quin Again

5: August

QUIN'S HERE. Quin has arrived in town. Yes, at long last Quin is here. I know it. The town knows it. I was sitting on a bench on the esplanade idly watching the beach below. The blue wrapping from a chocolate bar lay on the ground nearby. Without warning it stirred into action. It began to hop towards the rust-pitted railings which guard the five metre drop to the shingle. It reached the edge and jumped and was gone from my dying. There was no wind. In the same instant a group of gulls came tearing past, loudly screeching. Quin had just arrived and the town *knew*. The sea, tranquil a moment earlier, began to break into wild horses. A yacht began to swing round. The sailors ran to the rear and began to make adjustments.

I heard the rattle of brittle leaves scratching the rough esplanade path. I heard the bass thump of music from what might have been a passing car. A repetitive thudding. But there was no such vehicle visible and I knew what it was. It was Quin's massive heart. I could hear each muddy beat. Her pulse animated the unspaces. Her own excitement quickened as her high heels clacked along the platform. She knew it would not take long to track me down. She would have at her disposal the latest technology. Not just the surveillance wasps. Not just blue fly trackers. Not just whisper moths. Not just synthetic tracker cats. She'd have Company stardust, Company speedworms, Company blood finders. The DNA hover needles would already have been released into the bracing seaside air. I could smell Quin's excitement. A trickle of salt bled from each shaved armpit. The talcum powder muskiness of her skin and the acrid perfume from le deuxième arrondissement cannot conceal her imminence from me. She was tangibly within a mile. She was, I guessed, just off the afternoon train. Quin had always favoured the slowest of locomotion. Her mind abhorred speed. Her intutions roosted in slowly passing fields, the glide of muddy glinting estuaries. And then I lose her. She is passing among buildings, beyond my radar. But I need not worry. It is only a matter of time, our meeting.

Quin has been here a whole day, now. But she has yet to make a move. She is invisible. She leaves me messages. Hints, texts, arrangements of cloud. She knows my expertise in codes. She knows I can decipher her scatterings, her tiny teases.

Did I say this before? I no longer remember. I first met Quin in a very hot summer during the last century. She appeared in a nearby doorway, shimmering. She was soaked to the skin. At first I thought she was nude but this was simply a trick of the light. She wore a flesh-coloured outfit and the yellow fooled me. Or did she emerge down there, where the wind howls and the sand dances? Did she come from the sea? In truth, I no longer remember. All I know is that once we were one, until she split.

Veronika has nothing to do with any of this, really. I say that even though I am drawn here by Veronika Freie. Vee, I called her. Vee whom I did not begin to love until she was dead. Vee who meant sex at a time when sex was what mattered to me. Vee who was astonishingly beautiful, with hair that came down to her waist.

Blue was the colour of the sky on the day of Vee's incineration. I did not like the priest. He was Welsh and continually seeped grease. His pitch grated. The insincerity of his sincerity was palpable. Half the time I had no idea who this Veronika was he simpered about. She was half saint, half caring daughter. The vast chapel was as unpleasant as a cold examination hall to an eleven-year-old. The benches accommodated two hundred and were not needed for our little huddle of grief. Half way through the funeral service a door at the back suddenly slammed, like in a horror film. I could hear distant traffic and the cooing of pigeons. The Nilsson song which played as the coffin rolled away was my last punishment. Vee bought it when I left her for Quin. Her brother had the full story. Grimly he laid his narrative upon me. He was a banker. I bowed my head solemnly, attentively. It would have been coarse to be impolite. I never liked Phil. I knew I would never again see Vee's widowed mother or Phil and I never have done. Mother is probably dead by now. She was an elegant woman, very tall and slim, with exquisite cheekbones. Vee had always wanted to punish her mother in a way I never understood. While her mother sat downstairs in her lounge talking to the gardener, Vee insisted we fuck at the top of the stairs. While her mother sat in a deckchair reading a magazine, Vee lay behind the rhododendron, took off her knickers, and opened her legs. While her mother clattered pans in the kitchen we copulated in the bathroom with the door open. Her mother declined to engage her daughter in battle. Her poise and calm were magnificent. Perhaps she was a secret Buddhist. Vee's brother, by contrast, seemed smooth and empty. Mike, Pete, Dick, his name I cannot quite remember. It was something monosyllabic and banal. He bobbed at the edges of our passion. I have never liked bankers or barristers or politicians. I much prefer the company of musicians, playwrights and assassins.

'I am afraid you are a very sick man,' my psychiatrist said. She added: 'I have arranged for us to have a day out together. In my car. Dr Martin does not approve but he does not wish to alienate me.' Her smile was provocative yet tender. 'I shall bring my handcuffs,' she said. 'I have booked a room at a motel. The room has mirrors, many mirrors.' 'I look forward to it, Dr Quin.'

So, this is the end. No more words, old friend. I am done with words. I am left with all that's left to me. Strips of shingle and sand wedged between crumbling cliffs and the dark North Sea. Milena D'eath? I knew her well in the old days. That surprises you, does it not? But it's true. I used to know her. And I always believed we'd meet again some day. I shall stop pretending she was called Gotz. Her name was and is and always will be Milena D'eath. And if you believe that you are as gullible as my shrink. Sincerely, Cliff Tollinger.

Yes, I am done with words. But words are not done with me.

Today I'll go on. I am not quite dead yet. This old dog can still wag his pitiful tail. Today I am listening to 'When the Stars Go Blue'. An old Ryan Adams number. After that 'Blue', sung by Lucinda Williams. Just now as I was staring out of the window, thinking of Gotz, a gull flew past unexpectedly. It was early morning and frost coated the grass and the windows of the cars parked in the street. The sky was powder blue, the light a little unearthly. I was startled by the sudden appearance of the gull, by its speed and by its colouring. The first rays of the risen sun had transformed its breast and wings into gold. I am not going to use the word 'angelic'.

Quin Again

Before our meeting happens I am going back to a ruined room, thistles, a particular boulder.

Too late.

Quin appeared when least expected. We held our first conversation for many, many years. 'I am afraid, my love, that you are under an illusion in thinking you can terminate me.' 'And why is that?' 'It's perfectly simple, really. I am already dead. You killed me a while back. I have a record of it. Look, I have it written down. August 26th. That was the day you killed me.' 'What year was that? It wasn't this year because I was in Bristol then. And the year before that I was in New York. And the year before that I was in New Hampshire. And the year before that I was in Berlin. And before that I was on Acadia Road. In fact I was on Acadia Road for many, many years. I remember it well. It was a pink apartment block. I lived on the top floor.' 'My love, you know which year it was. I do not need to spell it out to you.' 'But if, as you say, you are already dead, then what I am doing here?' 'I would have thought that was obvious,' I said. I had the knife in my right hand. It was nothing special – a cheap cutting knife bought from the local supermarket. I brought it up from below the table and forced it through her blouse. I was aiming for her heart. I do not know how well I succeeded, as anatomy was never one of my best subjects. I pushed the knife in as hard as I could and then twisted it. Quin winced a little and gave a little groan. I was reminded of our ancient lovemaking. But then my hand was hit by hot, wet splashes. I did not look down, so I do not know whether it was her tears or her blood. Besides, it did not seem to matter. 'You have killed me,' she whispered. 'But this also is not possible,' I said. I was buoyant with explanations now. Everything was very bright and very clear. The dark, dingy room was filled with shining light. 'You see you killed me on a Thursday. I remember it was about ten o'clock in the morning. But I did not die at once. I lingered on for some time. I remember I was in great pain. Somehow I managed to crawl home. My heart was squirting blood and I was starting to lose all feeling in my body. I found a sheet of paper and dipped my finger in my heart's blood and wrote your name. QUIN, I wrote. She KILLED me. She FINISHED me off. I wanted to establish the facts. I put stamps on the envelope. I found my way to a pillar box. I held on to it like a lover. I smeared it in my blood but it did not seem to matter as it was already the colour of my deep wound. I managed to get the letter into the slit. I went back home and lay down on the bed. I say bed but I do not think there was one. I think there was a sleeping roll. The floor was greasy. I remember a sink and a pair of taps. I remember a small window and a view down to a dark yard of concrete with three dustbins. And there I died.'

Correction. I died in the cemetery outside Tongue, the one just before the causeway. I went back there, alone. I swallowed pills, many pills. I drank down a bottle of whisky, like in the old days. I took out the knife and sliced through my veins. And there I lay down to die. I didn't want to go on. I didn't want her to drive me south, where her husband was waiting. I wanted it all to be over and done with, right there.

'Afterwards,' I said, 'I decided I might as well come back and live on the coast. I knew one day you'd join me. I always dreamed we'd settle down together, just the two of us. Two old corpses. Embalming fluid would leak from our embrace. Fluid would drip from each cold kiss. We might manage a kiss. We'll go no more a-roving but we might manage a kiss.'

I say, I say, I say! Did I mention how blue is how it is around here? Did I say that blue is where it ends? Yes, the end is coming and no mistake. Rock of ages, cleft for me. Let me hide myself in Thee.

August 26, 1pm.

Here I sit reading, imagining that your eyes will rest on the same pages. I am drinking gin and tonic and my Love, my Love, my Love, I am so full of your presence that my eyes keep brimming over and I hear your voice in my ears and feel your hands on my body and all the words I say express only a minute fraction of what I feel. I have thought a thousand times that I am the luckiest woman under the sun because you love me.

Quin wrote that.

And Quin wrote this.

Where are you now, my Love? Walking along a street? I followed you with my eyes when you walked away through the crowd and I wanted to run after you and then people pushed me on... All I could think of then was the moment when I will see you emerging from a door or a crowd. My Love, I am disjointed and my thoughts whirl through my head. One thing I know – that my love for you is rooted in my heart for as long as I breathe.

After she wrote those words I never saw Quin again.

Quin has been here a whole day, now. But she has yet to make a move. She is invisible. She leaves me messages. Hints, texts, arrangements of cloud. She knows my expertise in codes. She knows I can decipher her scatterings, her tiny teases. I am returning to Quin. I can hear her breathing in the night. She is getting closer.

A woman named Gotz, who changed her name to Quin, came to a seaside town carrying a knife... And I don't mind at all. I am tired of running from her. I'm exhausted. I'm finished. I am done with words. And I know this is all going to end in a way that is unimaginable.

www.ingramcontent.com/pod-product-compliance
Lightning Source LLC
Chambersburg PA
CBHW020410150626
46554CB00012B/560